THE GOLDEN WARRIOR

The warrior born from the flames of fire!

Naveen Rajaka

Leadstart
INKSTATE

ISBN 978-93-54582-75-2
Copyright © Naveen Rajaka, 2021

First published in India 2021 by Leadstart Inkstate
A brand of One Point Six Technologies Pvt. Ltd.

123, Building J2, Shram Seva Premises,
Wadala Truck Terminal,
Mumbai 400022, Maharashtra, INDIA
Phone: +91 96999 33000
Email: info@leadstartcorp.com
www.leadstartcorp.com

Disclaimer This is a work of fiction. All the names, characters, businesses, places, events and incidents in this book are either the product of the author's imagination or used in a fictitious manner. Any resemblance to actual persons, living or dead, or actual events is purely coincidental.

Editor: Sanjhee Gianchandani
Cover: R. Maharaja
Layouts: Kshitij Dhawale

ACKNOWLEDGEMENTS

I would like to acknowledge my little brother Tharun for inspiring me with this novel. I would also thank my Mom and Dad on this project. I thank the entire Leadstart Publications team for working with me on this book.

ABOUT THE AUTHOR

Naveen is a sales executive working in a stock broking company. He is an avid reader and writes novels in his free time. He writes majorly on novels that give people hope. He also likes making YouTube videos on personality development and motivation. His writings are majorly for kids although even adults can enjoy reading his novels.

Tears rolled down through Agathashatru's cheeks as he held his dying master. The grand old Master was painfully coughing blood from his mouth trying to tell Agathashatru how to find the warrior born from the flames of fire.

The fire was devouring everything around them. It was a dark night and was made even darker by all the sinister things that had happened today. Dead headless bodies were all around them.

Grand Master spoke painfully struggling against pain, 'A-Agathashatru…people with selfish desires and evil intentions will rise again!' taking some breath he continued, 'Only the warrior born from the flames of fire can stop them. I am trusting you with this task.'

Agathashatru replied heaving with tears, 'Master?! Where will I find him?'

Grand Master knew his body was nearing its mortal end. The final mantra he used to stop the ritual demanded his death. Grand Master chose death instead of allowing the ritual to complete. In his dying moments, he knew it was far from over. It was only the beginning of a tragedy that he has to stop by revealing the truth to Agathashatru.

He echoed his answer in monotonous syllables, 'You…find him… will come…you searching for him...Recognise him...'

Agathashatru did not understand his Master's broken statement. 'Master? Tell me more about how to find him?'

He clanged to his Master's body which was now still. The Master's chest was not heaving anymore. His eyes were fixated in one direction. All his muscles were relaxed. The Master died.

Fresh tears were rolling down from Agathashatru's eyes. He knew it was his doing. He was the one responsible for all the deaths that happened that night and the ones that would happen in centuries to come.

More Than 1000 years later…

CHAPTER 1

Vyom was very worried as he guided the tourists around the jungle. They were foreigners and they demanded to explore the jungle. They were paying him good money and so he had accepted it.

He just had to wait till the morning and he would receive his final payment to settle the debt his father had incurred to raise him.

The waterfall was refreshingly new. Jacob and his friends wanted some delicious adventure on vacation and it seems they arrived at the right location. Their guide Vyom has been very helpful in making them understand the historical significance of this place. Olivia, Jacob's girlfriend was lost at the spectre of the Waterfall. The sound of water smashing at the rocks, cool breeze flowing from the trees, little birds singing their melodious songs; it was all very enrapturing.

Emily and Ethan were kissing each other on the opposite side of the waterfall. While Logan was trying to communicate something with the birds.

Jacob and his four companions along with their guide Vyom were the only people who had dared to explore this deep into the forest. No one else was to be seen there.

After the full-day exploration at the Waterfall and the surrounding jungle, Jacob and his friends arrived at the end of their journey. It was beginning to get dark when Olivia saw to the far east a palace-like mansion.

'What's that structure over there?' Olivia asked Jacob.

'That is the dreaded mansion!' Vyom answered with stillness in his voice.

'Dreaded Mansion?!' Ethan questioned.

Jacob noticed the obvious unease Vyom was experiencing at the sight of the Old Mansion. He was sweating at the mere sight of that mansion.

With great effort Vyom changed the topic, 'I suggest we all get back to your lodgings.'

'Surely we would. But after we explore that old mansion' Emily said.

'There is nothing to explore there. It is just an old broken mansion.' Vyom answered angrily. 'You asked me to guide you to the waterfalls, I did. Now let's get back.'

'But why did you say it was the Dreaded Mansion?' Logan asked hesitatingly.

Vyom realised by the faces of his tourists that they were interested in knowing the past of that dreaded mansion. He thought it best that he tells them the legend behind the mansion to satisfy their curiosity and move back to their hotel. They had already arrived too deep into the jungle now.

'The dreaded mansion,' Vyom began, 'is the hiding place of evil Tantrics.'

'What is Tantrics?' Emily asked.

'Tantrics are equivalent to Western witches who practise the dark arts and use it against people for their evil purposes. Anyone who comes into contact with them does not see the light of the day. They remain in hiding in the deepest recesses of the jungle. Anyone who has entered their hiding place never came back.'

'You mean to say that mansion is haunted?' Olivia blinked in disbelief.

'All I know is that no local folk dares to go there,' replied Vyom, 'As per the local legends a terrible Tantric is imprisoned in that mansion for his gruesome deeds. Local legend also has it that Tantric is the master of all the dark arts. And his presence is feared by one and all.'

'Sounds interesting! I think we should visit that mansion.' Emily said, her curiosity getting the better of her.

'No!' Vyom said firmly. 'Nothing is interesting about that place. You have come here as tourists and as your guide, I request you to get back to your hotel. It's already getting dark here.'

Logan was scared of all the narrative Vyom presented before him. Logan said in half soft and half scared voice, 'If he says that it is not worth visiting then we should move back to our hotel. We have no business down there. We already explored the waterfall and the adjoining jungle.'

Jacob agreed, 'Yes! Vyom is our guide and he knows this place better than any of us. If he insists, we go back that is what we should do.'

Emily dug at Jacob, 'Jacob, don't tell me you are afraid of an old mansion or the stories of evil witches or Tantrics.'

'I am not afraid' Jacob tried to counter when Olivia interrupted him, 'Jacob let's go there. These haunted stories are just local tales. They are superstitious people. Don't we know better?'

Jacob found it difficult to say no to Olivia. Jacob turned towards

Vyom for his opinion.

Vyom nodded his head in disagreement, 'I have never come this far in the jungle. No guide or person dares to come into this dense jungle, let alone going near that mansion. All the locals stray far from it for some reason.'

But Olivia and Emily were both insistent on going there. Jacob finally made up his mind and decided to go to the mansion.

Vyom was adamant about not going there. Jacob simply doubled the amount he would pay Vyom for guiding them there.

The mention of double the amount had caused the greed in Vyom to overcome his fear for that mansion. He agreed.

Upon reaching the outskirts of the mansion, Vyom immediately regretted his decision. The whole place had a foreboding look upon it as a cemetery. The mansion was crumbling under twisted trees. There was no sign of any life anywhere near the mansion. No creature big or small was to be found. Distant sounds of owls hooting in the night were audible. The cooing of different birds only added to the gruesome appearance of the mansion.

The gates of the mansion were huge. Still more gigantic than the gates was the mansion itself. The path that led from the gates to the doors of the mansion was covered with dead grass.

Vyom along with his tourists opened the closed gates. The metal sound of gates creaking open was in stark contrast with the sound of the waterfall they had listened to just a couple of hours ago.

Logan could feel in the pit of his stomach that they should go away from there. But no one would listen to him.

Jacob felt a gentle touch on his head. He saw upwards, it had started to rain gently.

They arrived at the door of the mansion and it was erringly strange. The door of the mansion was designed like a devil opening his mouth with fang-like teeth on both sides. Jacob pushed open the door. Cobwebs were torn by the opening of the door.

They started coughing as the dust flew into their mouths. Outside the rain was now pouring heavily. The full moon was now rising. Wolves were howling in the rain and at the sight of the full moon. Their howls sent a wave of chill to Vyom.

The mansion was not like anything they had seen. The sheer gigantism of the mansion with huge corridors was overwhelming. Olivia felt as if she was in a Disney Castle, except the mansion was very old.

They observed one particular thing in the mansion: Stone statues. There were stone statues all around them covered in cobwebs of immense size and structure. Jacob went to a nearby stone statue and stared at it. It was a statue that was made up of stone but the face was like a living human. Whoever made these stone statues must be a master sculpture, Jacob felt. Even the swords in the hands of the statue along with their dressings were of pure stone. Jacob wondered how someone could sculpt such a difficult structure with such unerring accuracy.

Meanwhile, others were occupied in their spectre. 'Jacob!' Olivia screamed. Jacob looked in the direction of Olivia. She was visibly over ecstatic. Jacob reached near the others when Olivia pointed upwards.

There in the middle of the corridors of the mansion was another statue levitating in the air with no support whatsoever. The construction of the statue was bizarre in itself. The statue was looking at his own hands. The facial expressions of the statue were that of someone who was screaming at his fate looking at his hands. Olivia took a careful look at the statue's face. The eyes of the statue caught Olivia's attention. Olivia could read intense hatred in the statue's eyes.

Jacob similarly noticed that all the facial expressions of all the statues were filled with equal hatred and rage.

'How could a statue levitate in mid-air?' Emily spoke up.

No one had any answer to it.

'Tantric Magic!' Vyom replied.

Logan ventured a little further than the others without noticing the grotesque levitating statue. Though scared, Logan was mesmerized by the mansion and its anachronous contents. The large windows out of which rain was splashing in and out. The long curtains which seemed centuries old had still maintained their original reddish colour. The longer he walked the bigger the mansion seemed to get. The mansion was much bigger than what they had assumed at first sight.

To the side of the curtain was an immense stone statue of a giant man with a chopper like weapon in his hand. His body was clouded in the armour of stone. Something about the statue attracted Logan towards it just when he heard Shrieks of Olivia and Emily.

Just when Vyom answered, 'Tantric Magic!' there was a deathly chill everywhere. The full moon had now risen to its full peak and wolves and jackals were howling with all their might. The rain started bursting with even greater force. Owls were hooting in the night.

As the rays of the full moon fell upon the mansion for a brief moment the whole mansion shone with unbearable light. The rays of the moon fell on the levitating stone statue through the window. Little by little, Vyom witnessed the horror of what was happening before him. The legend he had heard since childhood was now realising before his own eyes.

Jacob, Olivia, Emily, and Ethan were transfixed upon the levitating stone statue. As the rays of the moon covered the entire statue, it turned into pure flesh.

Logan could see from a distance that the statue in mid-air was transforming into a living breathing man. A dark aura was accumulating around the mid-air statue.

The transformation was now complete. The man jumped to the ground heaving for air. He could feel the air going in and out from his chest. He slowly touched his face and felt the softness of his skin and the warmth of his body returned. His hair was ruffling in the strong air from the window. Once again Charvik felt alive.

In front of him, he saw uninvited guests who had trespassed his mansion. They were comparatively small in size. He could see the fear in their eyes and their bodies. He turned his head in one full circle and smiled wickedly at his guests.

Olivia's initial judgments about him were correct. His eyes were bloodred. And she could see quite clearly the infinite hatred he felt for others, not like him. Cold-blooded remorseless eyes. Eyes that abhorred joy of any sort. Eyes who could enjoy only when others were suffering. Eyes that felt no kinship with others. Eyes that felt repulsion just by looking at others.

Vyom was trembling at the sight of Charvik. He could see death dancing in the eyes of the man who had just turned from stone to man.

From a distance, Logan was shaking in horror at the entire spectre when he felt a long shadow fall over him. He turned around. The shadow was of the statue he had been looking at a little while ago except it was not a statue anymore.

The gigantic frame of the man holding a weapon ten times the size of a chopper was enough to terrify Logan. The expression on that man's face only added to the terror Logan was experiencing. The expression was that of a butcher looking at his prey one final time before slaughtering it.

Logan and his friends looked around and they saw all the stone statues were turned to life. All of them had a hostile expression on their faces.

It was raining in the night while a couple of owls were feasting on a rat. They recoiled in fear as they heard screams of pain as if someone was being butchered alive from the mansion. Their instincts told them to abandon their feast and take flight away from the mansion. And so, they did.

In his final moment, Jacob remembered what his guide Vyom said some hours ago, 'Anyone who comes in contact with them does not see the light of the day.' He now knew it was true.

CHAPTER 2

The little girl was out of breath as she ran towards her destination. She had to get there fast before it was too late.

The forest was dense. Without any footwear, the girl was running with bruises on her feet. She had to get to the tantrics and seek their help to save her father.

Agathashatru started coming out as fast as his aching feet allowed him. His face was full of wrinkles with tired and weary eyes. He wore a black cloak that covered his frail body. With thin arms and hands. His wrists and ankles were adorned with bracelets with mystic symbols.

His second in command Swethakethu has just informed him that a small girl was found near the woods and her pulse was not beating. Agathashatru wanted to reach there promptly so that he can do something for the girl.

It was the first time in 300 years that he had stepped out from his residing place. The rays of the sun fell upon his face, he tried to adjust his eyes to the light of the day. So much time had elapsed that he felt the warmth of the sun on his skin. Sun was at its peak and heat was unbearable yet holding his caretaker, Yajin's hand he balanced himself.

Yajin was a young tantric taking his tuitions under his Grand Master Agathashatru himself. Thin built but of strong will and a fast-learner, devotedly attached to all his tantric teachers. Quite at a young age, he had mastered so many tantric mantra's. Agathashatru was impressed by the boy's capabilities.

Jatasya rushed to held Agathashatru at the stairs. Agathashatru saw Jatasya and recalled just how fast the time has fled him by. It appeared like only yesterday when he had enrolled Jatasya as a young boy for the tantric learnings and now he was a middle-aged man.

'Master!' Jatasya comforted.

Agathashatru asked, 'What happened to the girl?'

'She is dead,' Jatasya articulated, 'It seems she tried coming to us. She was alone. We found she was holding a piece of cloth torn from her frock with a message for help.'

'What message?' Agathashatru questioned.

A large black coloured Owl came from the sky and landed on Yajin's shoulder. The Owl was Onik, it was the pet owl of Agathashatru.

'A message begging for help!' Swethaketu answered in anger and showed the fragment of the cloth to Agathashatru.

Agathashatru held the fragmented piece of cloth in his right hand. It was written in blood. Only a few words were written- 'Please save my Papa.' Placing the piece of cloth on the palm of his right hand, he swiped his left hand over it.

His black eyes turned bloodred. He could envision the little girl who fell on the deserted land exasperated without water. The girl was tired and left without energy, gave up in her efforts to find the tantrics. Her legs and body were in pain, the sun was at its peak with blistering heat sucking little by little the life out of the girl. In the last dig of effort to help her father, she tore a piece of her frock. Cut herself in the hand with an incisive metal and wrote the message-Please save my Papa.

Agathashatru realized that the poor girl was coming to them to ask for help. Agathashatru envisioned once again, his eyes turned bloodred. He could see that the girls' father was being held captive by the king in the nearest kingdom for a minor error. The girl's father was a servant to the king. Just because he fell ill and was not able to come to the service of the king, the king ordered his death. Upon learning the fate of her father, she approached the elderly people in her kingdom for help. None came forward but one old aged woman with bent curve told her that she had heard legends from her parents that tantrics are living beyond the mountain. And in search of the tantrics, she came this far.

Chandramauli along with his disciples came forward carrying the little lifeless body of the girl. It pained Agathashatru, he frowned in agony at the body of the little girl. She tried coming to him seeking his help and met with her untimely demise. He held the girls face; it was a pretty face now cold and lifeless. He held her hand and tried feeling her pulse, no use, she died.

At least he could save her father. Agathashatru along with Swethaketu, Jatasya, Chandramauli, and Yajin, set out to free the girl's father.

The news of the Tantrics arrival reached King Navendu.

'King Navendu! The tantrics are not someone we should be messing up with!' cautioned his minister Madhusoodan.

'Tantrics! They are ancient folk tales!' bemoaned the king Navendu. His other ministers were proudly laughing at the king's demeaning demeanour.

Madhusudan was an experienced old man. With white hair and a long flourishing beard stretching up to his chest. He tried to reign the king on his impulsive sadistic behaviour but the king only made fun of him along with his yes-saying ministers. And now the king despite his warnings was not serious about the tantrics either. All the childhood tales, Madhusoodan's elders told him about the tantrics was ringing in his ears. Things tantrics would do if their demands were not met. Things riddled with unspeakable horror. Things associated with unimaginable terror. Tantrics usually live on their own but when they arrive, death always comes with them. They were best left alone.

Agathashatru and his disciples reached the king's grand palace. It was a tall structure with grandeur associated with it. They noticed all around the palace people where were trying to hide out from their way. The legend of the tantrics was still popular despite there being not active for so long.

They made their way into the court of the palace. Ministers were seated on either side of it with the king sitting on his throne. Servants and slaves were doing the cleansing works of the palace. The owl, Onik was scanning the strange new place.

'Servants! Clean the palace once again as it got muddied by the entrance of these despicable beings!' insulted the king Navendu. The king's supportive ministers howled with laughter at the insulting remark.

'King Navendu! We should be polite with the tantrics!' suggested Madhusoodan. Madhusudan took a careful look at the tantrics before him. They were five of them in total with a black coloured owl. One very old man, obviously the Grand Master. Two old people who must be in their early fifties. One man who was in his thirties and a young teenage boy.

The king dismissed his plea. And talked to the group of people before him who were dressed in black.

'What is it that you want?' King Navendu asked in a humiliating tone.

Agathashatru stepped forward and looked around the gigantic court with ministers sneering down at him. He requested, 'King Navendu, please release this little girl's father. She came to us for help but died in the heat.'

The body of the little girl was brought before the king. The king looked at the body with displeasure. He remembered the girl; she had already begged him for releasing her father but he did not heed it.

'That man shall die for not informing the royal court about his absence.' The king thundered.

'Wise King' Agathashtru said, 'Please forgave the man. He already lost his daughter. No punishment can be as hard for a man as seeing his loving daughter dead.'

'I can forgive the man if you touch my feet!' insulted the king.

At his comment, his ministers started their derisive laughter once again. Agathashatru was aghast! He knew the king has crossed his last line.

Yajin was visibly seething from the king's disdainful remarks. He did not have the patience that his elder tantrics had. He was continuously advised against impulsive actions. Yet he could not hold on more. The derisive laughter in the court at his Grand Masters expense was more than he could take. He ventured forward spelling something just when Jatasya gestured him to stop with his hands. Onik began to hoot as if in anger. Its hooting created a melancholy sound, something sinister was about to happen.

Madhasoodan observed that the young tantric boy was stopped by one of his elders. He knew it was not at all a good sign. The tantrics were nearing their boiling point. Whatever was about to happen would be horrendous. Madhusudan intervened out of sheer desperation, 'Maharaj! We should let the girl's father free. We have already punished him. Let us release him and end this matter!'

Agathashatru observed the wise mans' counsels but the king was not in the least bit interested in him or his counsels.

Agathashatru moved forward. 'If touching your feet will save that man, so be it.' Agathashatru frowned.

Yajin was getting more and more impatient by the minute. To see his grandmaster, touch the feet of the king was more than he could bear. Yet Jatasya, Swethaketu, and Chandramauli had not the least bit of expression on their faces. Their expressions were expressionless like a vulture scanning the vast landscape.

The laughter of the court ministers was now banging out all other noise at the spectacle before their eyes. Agathashatru bent forward on his one knee and placed his one hand on the king's foot as his command.

Madhusudan had never taught that tantrics would put their self-respect and dignity at someone else's foot. Perhaps they were not as powerful as he had been told.

Everyone taught that Agathashatru had touched the feet of the king. What no one saw was that Agathashatru had just held short of touching the king's feet and touched the ground or more appropriately the ground on which the king's shadow fell. For a brief moment, Agathashatru's black eyes turned bloodred and he was chanting some mystic verse.

'By the powers vested in me, I command the forces of nature to come to my aid. I command the flames to come to my aid. I command the silhouettes to come to my aid.'

No sooner had he said the mantra that the big banyan tree from the windows of the court lashed its branches out in every direction inside the court. Shadows of all the minister's guard even the king's shadow itself emerged from the ground. The heat began to rise and fires caught on the ground. Everything was under the consumption of fire except Madhusoodan and the few ministers who had advised the kings against his rash act.

Madhusudan was terror-struck at the visual before him. The king's shadow locked the king in his grip while all the other shadows began the slaughtering of its physical form. Aatreya the king's bodyguard tried to catch his shadow but all he could touch was thin air. While the shadow looked back at him with dark-black eyes.

The shadow thrust its shadowy sword into Aatreya and Aatreya fell holding his cut belly.

Yajin witnessed the entire episode with a strange feeling inside him. He now realized why the others were so serene when the Grandmaster was being insulted at. He realized they all already knew how this would end.

Meanwhile, the king who was held by his shadow started to squeak like caught prey. Agathashatru slowly went near him. Looking at all the massive grandeur being turned to ashes by fire and said, 'Such royalty and still so low at heart.' He uttered one syllable and the shadow twisted the king's head in one full rotation!'

After the slaughter was complete. Agathashatru held the fallen crown in his hand and looked at Madhusoodan.

He went near him. Madhusudan was not sure what Agathashatru's intentions were. Agathashatru placed the crown on Madhusoodan's head and said, 'You seem to be a wise man. Govern wisely.'

Saying so, Agathashatru and his band of disciples left the palace.

CHAPTER 3

It was a bright new morning. Leaves were still wet by the morning dew. The air was cool and the sun was just on his way up. Little birds were adding music to the day by their chirping. Two tiny squirrels were playing with each other for a nut.

The entire woods had beautiful scenery to it. The grass beneath the feet was soft and squeezy. Erish fell upon the ground, slipping his feet on the wet grass.

Erish got up on his two little tiny legs. He picked up his tiny little wooden sword, which was quite a bit in size for him. And started attacking the scarecrow which was suspended from the branch of the tree.

Erish was eight years old. His cheeks were chubby. And he had a bit of a stomach that was tummy. He had tiny little legs. He wore a simple brown shirt and a matching half pant. His eyes were round and bright. He was gifted with cuteness like all small children.

But that pretty little child had one grotesque thing. His right hand was twisted towards his chest. It was a birth defect. In light of his useless right hand, Erish mastered his left hand. Or perhaps he did not care about having another hand when he was so happy attacking the scarecrow with his perfect left hand.

'I am going to defeat you, you evil monster!' said Erish to the scarecrow.

In Erish's imagination, he was the warrior prince who would defeat the evil scarecrow man. He swung his wooden sword at the suspended scarecrow throwing the scarecrow up and down, right and left with his attacks.

Two birds were watching Erish's antics from the nearby branch. Just when Asmi came running towards her little brother Erish.

Asmi was twelve years old. She wore a snow-white frock. Her hair was tied up in ponytail style. She came rushing towards Erish. Erish saw her and tried to escape from there before Asmi could catch him. He grabbed his sword and started running but Asmi caught up with him in no time. She snatched his Sword and held him tight.

Erish protested, 'I want to play some more, I am just about to defeat the evil scarecrow man.'

'You can defeat the evil scarecrow man later. We have to return to school.' Asmi replied.

'I don't want to go to school. I want to play. Today is a holiday.' Erish protested

'Today is not a holiday. Today is Raksha Bandhan.' Asmi Countered.

Asmi picked Erish with all her might. Erish tried to wiggle away from her hands. Erish was a little fat as well adding to his sister's dilemma. But Asmi held Erish in a firm grip and carried him away to the School. Little Erish tried to wriggle himself free but to no avail.

The Sun was rising high in the sky. Its rays were entering the mansion through the window.

Charvik stepped into the light for the first time in three hundred years. A breeze of wind ruffled his long hair. He closed his eyes and took a deep breath and savoured the air in his lung, he felt the heat of the sun on his skin and relished it.

His second in command- Mahakethu was just a few feet away from him along with the rest of their lot.

Everybody was silent watching their leader lost in some thought.

Flashes of memories came back to Charvik, how he was treated by his people, by his father. The Pain, the anguish, the seething everything was still there. He will have his revenge completed soon, very soon.

Charvik brought his two hands two his head and massaged his way through till his neck. Then opened his eyes. He saw an eagle was seated in front of the branch before him feasting on a snake.

Charviks's second in command- Mahakethu came a bit closer. The rays of the Sun had cast a long shadow of Charvik. Mahakethu looked at the Shadow and saw two glittering dark red eyes were looking back at him. It was as if his shadow had a life of its own. But Mahakethu knew it was one of Charvik's many gifts that he could use his shadow for other purposes. He had seen this shadow glittering with eyes many times before but always had an unsettling feeling about it.

'So, when will we complete the Final Ritual?' Mahakethu asked.

'We will complete the Final Ritual in about a fortnight,' Charvik said without looking back. He was focused on the eagle eating the snake. 'We will require sacrifices.'

Charvik raised his hand in the direction of the Eagle. Formed a fist and uttered, 'By the powers vested in me, I take charge of you!' His eyes turned redder and darker. A light glowed from his hand and the next moment the eagle raised his head towards Charvik. It dropped its prey and came flying and stood on Charvik's outstretched arm.

Charvik was running his hands over the Eagle. Its eyes were blood red.

'We will go in search of sacrifices.'

 Erish and Asmi reached their school.

'The Orphanage School for Handicapped Children' was mentioned on the entry board of the school. The school was a giant monolithic structure built of white marble.

The design and dome of the school were made in medieval times. Covered all over by grass and greenery. It was as old as one could remember. Built specifically for the handicapped and orphanage children. It was maintained by several Old people headed by the school's headmaster

Kids with all sorts of handicaps were playing on the school fields. A one-legged boy who balanced himself with the help of a supporter came rushing towards Erish to play.

The Headmaster interrupted, 'You both can play later. Soon the celebrations of Rakshabandan would commence.'

Erish looked upwards to the Headmaster who was just behind him.

Erish questioned, 'What is Rakshabandan?'

'Hmm..!' The Headmaster amusedly replied, 'Raksha Bandhan is a festival to celebrate the bond between a brother and sister.'

Erish's head was full of confusion. The Headmaster looked at him and simplified it for him, 'It so happened that when a lady was in dire need of help no one came to her rescue. So, she went to a person she knew could help her. She tied him a Rakhi and asked him to accept her as his sister and protect her. The man accepted the lady as her sister and protected her from trouble. From that day onwards it was known famously as Rakshabandan: The bond of rescuing. So, a man should always rescue his sister from whatever trouble befell her. That's the story of Raksha Bandhan.'

'So Asmi would tie me a Rakhi?' Erish asked.

'Yes!'

'And I would be required to save her from whatever trouble befell her?'

'That's correct as well.'

Erish was scratching his head in assimilating this idea. He muttered, ' Well okay.'

After some time, all the brothers and their respective sisters were lined up in the corridors to celebrate the festival of Raksha Bandhan. Those girls who did not have brothers simply tied it to those boys who did not have any sister of their own.

And so, with buzzing music in the great hall of the school, all the sisters started to tie their self-made Rakhi to their brothers.

Asmi had made a Rakhi with the help of flowers and some stitches. She asked Erish to forward his hand. Erish forward his left hand as usual. She denied that hand and said that Rakhi was supposed to be tied only on the right hand.

Erish looked at his twisted Right hand. And he tried forwarding it but with no success. Finally, Asmi bent forward and tied the Rakhi on the Twister arm of Erish. Erish looked at the Rakhi on his hand and smiled.

Asmi then thrust the favourite sweet of Erish in his mouth and Erish ate it all gleefully.

The Sun was descending slowly. When Erish's friend spotted something on the outside of the sky.

He exclaimed, 'Whoa!'

Soon all the kids gathered around the windows to the school corridor to look at the spectacle in the sky.

Erish too came running to witness the spectacle outside on the insistence of his friend. Erish saw a flock of giant birds approaching the school from the distant sky.

These were gigantic eagles and vultures coming in hordes. Erish had never before seen these flocks of birds together. What was more astonishing was that these birds were not alone. They were saddled by a group of men.

Asmi came alongside Erish and started staring outside the window. The Outsiders were approaching nearer and nearer. The enormous birds landed on the school ground and the Outsiders stepped down from the birds.

Just then the dome of the school building blasted in a nanosecond. Rocks and soil were falling below. Many students and teachers alike were caught amid the debris.

Erish looked above the falling dome. It did not fell. One of the Outsiders was seated on a large vulture and he had somehow destroyed the school dome with a fire blast.

All the kids and teachers started running helter-skelter. The Outsiders soon stormed the school. Some school teachers tried stopping the Outsiders. One of them was Mr. Raghuveer, Erish's mathematics teacher. He had punched one of the Outsiders in the mouth. The punch did not injure the Outsider in the least bit.

The Outsider then raised his chopper right in the air and brought it down with a murderous force.

Asmi saw in horror as her Maths teacher was butchered in two pieces.

It was now apparent that the Outsiders wished them ill. The Outsiders started grabbing the kids tying them around the great bird's legs.

During the chaos, Asmi and Erish got separated.

'Erish! Erish!' Asmi was screaming from the crowd of the kids.

Erish was not able to locate Asmi in this mad crowd.

Then a swishing sound came across the school ground. Erish saw in the direction the swishing sound. Someone had made a fresh entry into the school ground. This was another Outsider on an eagle so big that it was nearly as big as the school.

An outsider had now landed from the gigantic eagle. It was Charvik.

Erish now turned his attention to find Asmi and to be with her.

Charvik was popping his fingers looking at the chaos before him. He caught an uncommon figure approaching him. Covered in lengthy red robes the school Headmaster approached the Outsiders.

One Outsider raised his chopper to butcher the Headmaster but the headmaster simply whispered, 'By the powers vested in me. Blast him away!' A fireball emerged from the Headmaster's hand and the Outsider has blasted a couple of yards away.

Charvik never thought he would find a tantric in a school. But in life, one should always anticipate unexpected contingencies. Charvik had witnessed it in his life.

The Headmaster was informed years ago that something like this was about to happen. He made preparations to deal with the upcoming problem but now he felt as if he had grossly underestimated the upcoming problem.

He looked at Charvik. He got the clarity instantly, finish this Outsider off the rest of them would scurry like scared rodents.

The Headmaster raised his hand towards Charvik. Charvik kept watching the headmaster closely without any emotion on his face.

The headmaster muttered, 'by the powers vested in me. Burn him down.'

The fire started throwing itself from the headmaster's hand. It engulfed Charvik burning all of his surroundings but not Charvik.

Headmaster held the fire for as long as he could to finish the principal Outsider. But he could sense despite being covered in flames the Outsider was not the least bit affected. The Headmaster tensed his muscles and roared in fury with all his being. The fire current emerged from his hand anew and started surrounding Charvik burning him down.

'By the powers vested in me. Explode him away.' Charvik muttered engulfed in fire.

The headmaster has exploded away from the force of Charvik's black fire. The headmaster collided against the wall and fell to the ground.

Charvik did not even cast a single look at the struggling body of the headmaster. He went inside to complete his final ritual.

The Outsiders were capturing the kids one by one and tying them off to the birds.

Charvik entered the school building. He saw a girl trying to push past the amassed crowd screaming, 'Erish! Erish!'

Charvik caught her from the backside of her hair and pulled her backward.

Erish managed to get on top of a small stool and started looking for Asmi. He saw that Charvik caught hold of Asmi and was now dragging her back to his great Eagle.

Asmi struggled against the hand of Charvik trying to free herself. She somehow managed to turn and bite the hand of Charvik.

Charvik was furious he tugged her head and smashed it against the strong pillar of the school. Asmi fell unconscious.

Erish stepped down from the stool and started to run to save Asmi.

Erish desperately ran towards Charvik and tried to bit his hand but Charvik caught hold of his shirt and picked him up to see him face to face.

Charvik saw the twisted arm of Erish and felt repugnant at it.

'We have captured 100 kids!' Mahakethu informed Charvik.

'In that case, we will not need this one,' Said Charvik, saying so, he threw Erish against the wall with force.

Erish collided with the wall and fell to the ground. The pain was searing in his head and body. The collision was painful. He tried to relieve his pain by rubbing his hand against it but it had little effect. Rocks, stones, and dust was falling everywhere as the school fell apart. Erish tried to cover himself against the rocks and stones by upholding his twisted arm but it did not provide enough cover.

Charvik placed Asmi on his vulture. She was still unconscious. Charvik climbed the Vulture and started taking off. All his followers followed suit. Mahakethu held two children in his arms and seated himself on his vulture.

Erish saw that they were about to take off. Asmi was still in their hold. He had to protect his sister soon.

He started running against the falling rocks and dust towards the stairs that led to the top terrace of the school. His limbs were aching with pain as he tried to climb the stairs as fast as he could. The stairs that were so perfect just a few hours ago were now in tatters. He had to place his feet on the proper spot because stairs started collapsing.

Just in front of him, he saw a big hole in the stairs and he had to make a big jump if he had to go to the other side. Using all his might and power in his tiny legs he made the jump.

He landed on the edge of the broken stairs half slipping and half trying to regain his balance on the stairs. Finally, he regained his balance and reached the top terrace of the school. Half the terrace was already gone because of the destruction caused by the outsiders. There was now a gigantic hole in the terrace from which all the outsiders could take off.

He witnessed all the outsiders rose in the air on their vultures. He tried desperately to search for Asmi. He scanned the outsiders there were so many of them to locate Asmi and the one who held her, the one whom the outsiders called Charvik.

The memory was still fresh in his mind when Charvik had picked him and looked at him. That feeling of hatred and repugnancy at his twisted arm and no care at all in his manners that man must surely be evil, Erish thought.

He looked for Asmi and Charvik but they were nowhere to be found.

Charvik was about to take off when the old man in red robes emerged once again.

'You will never succeed in your evil intentions.' The old man said.

'So many have said so yet here I am,' Charvik answered as matter-of-factly.

The old man in red robes prepared himself for another fight. He raised his arms and whispered a mantra. A bright red ball of fire was evolving from his hand.

Charvik saw the bright red ball of fire and it triggered a memory from his childhood. Charvik remembered the bright red ball of fire which his father taught to him when he was small. The very first mantra he had learned and mastered. The mantra that was the beginning of his quest and the end of his relationship with his father.

He remembered it vividly how lovingly his father had taught him all those powerful mantras. How good of a father he had and also how it all came crashing down.

The red ball of fire burst in Charvik's face and brought him back out of his reverie. The old man in red robes had attacked him with the ball of fire.

Charvik focused on the present moment and looked at the old man who wanted to still fight.

The Old man was flabbergasted half in fear and half in awe. He had attacked with his most powerful mantra and yet it did not leave a single bruise on its victim. How powerful can he be?

Charvik was enjoying the fear in the old man's eyes. He dropped down from the vulture and decided to give this old man a painful memory.

Charvik whispered a mantra and suddenly a big black ball of evil power emerged from his hand and he launched his attack on the old man.

The poor old man was no match before Charvik's powers. The ball of the fire pushed the old man out of the school into the playground. The old man was struggling to breathe and make sense of what was happening around him.

The old man could not believe how a beautiful day was ending as the worst nightmare of his life. He had vowed as the headmaster of the school to protect all his school children and he was failing in that oath. More painfully though was the fact that he would be also not able to keep the promise he made to his dead father for the first time in his life.

He still remembered that fateful day when his father dying on his deathbed held his son's hand in a loving fatherly way. His father was one of the noblest men he had ever known, he was always high spirited and high principled. He took the promise from his son. And after all these years his son was failing to keep his promise.

A long shadow fell over the old man and disturbed his past thoughts. The old man still lying on the ground in pain came a bit to his senses. He tried to see whose shadow had fallen on him. It was Charvik's.

Charvik came forward to the old man and looked into his eyes.

'I can kill you here and now but I won't. I want to gift you this day, this memory. The day where you were not able to protect your children. The day you failed. Do you want to know what I am planning to do with these kids of yours? Then hear me: I am going to butcher them one by one. All of them.' His voice was coarse and harsh. Full of hatred he continued, ' And you will live with this memory, this helplessness. That you tried and you failed. I want you to live with this regret for the rest of your miserable life.'

Saying so, Charvik departed from the old man towards his vulture where Asmi was still lying unconscious. He climbed on it. He looked above. His followers were still above him waiting for their master's arrival.

In one swift movement, he rose above to make his way out of the school's broken terrace.

Erish was still searching for Asmi and Charvik when Charvik

emerged from the hole in his school terrace.

Charvik did not notice Erish was standing and observing him along the edge of the terrace. He rose higher into the air.

Erish was exhausted, in pain, and at a loss for what to do. He knew that he had to protect his sister somehow or else he might never see her again. He searched his surroundings and found a big concrete rock near him.

He immediately picked it in his hand and aimed at Charvik's head. In one quick motion, he threw the stone at Charvik.

The stone missed its mark. Instead of hitting Charvik's head, he hit his shoulders.

Charvik looked in the direction from where the stone had hit him. And he saw the same boy with the twisted arm.

Erish was screaming in anger. 'Let her go. Let her go!'

Erish picked another stone and threw it once again at Charvik.

Charvik dodged the stone. Charvik's dark shadow came over him and for a brief but long moment, Erish saw the outsider for what he was like! He was completely dark with reddish eyes. A dark aura surrounded him and he felt like some sort of otherworldly being. Erish felt fear and stepped back a few steps.

Charvik felt like killing the kid then there but decided against it. He along with his followers took his flight away from the school. After all, what could a little boy with a twisted arm do?

Erish was screaming and roaring with all his might. But Charvik did not return.

Little did he knew then what could that little boy with the twisted arm can do.

CHAPTER 4

Erish ran towards the old man who lost consciousness after the fight with Charvik.

'Headmaster! Headmaster!' Erish tried waking his headmaster. Erish rubbed his headmaster's forehead and cheeks to bring some life into him.

Seeing nothing was happening of his actions, Erish rushed to the school well to fetch some water for the headmaster.

He poured the water into his headmaster's mouth and sprinkled some of the water on the headmaster's head.

The headmaster gasped for more water. Erish poured more of it. Little by little the headmaster opened his eyes and regained his consciousness.

With great effort, the headmaster tried getting up and sat upon the ground. The fight took too much strength away from the headmaster.

Erish silently saw the struggle and pain as his headmaster adjusted himself on the ground and started to make sense of what had just happened.

Erish had no understanding of what was going on but he knew that his headmaster knew something about what had just happened. He knew who the Outsider was and whatever it is that he wanted.

Erish asked his headmaster, 'Headmaster who was that Outsider, and Why did he take Asmi and all my friends?'

The headmaster was still and lost in some thought when Erish's question brought him back to the present.

He looked at Erish, the boy who wanted and tried to save his sister. The boy was half scared about the Outsiders and half-eager to save his sister.

The Headmaster tried to stand up on his feet. Erish handed him support in getting up from the ground.

The School and the school ground were wreaked havoc. Other kids who had escaped the Outsiders clutches were frightened to death. Even the school teachers were pale at the horror of what has happened. Still, the school teachers tried to console the crying children and started taking them to their respective dorms unaware of what to do.

'Who were they? And what is it that they wanted?', 'Where did they took our school children?', 'What are we supposed to do now?', ' We have to bring all those children safely and securely back to school!'

The school teachers and the headmaster were discussing the ongoing things to be done. All of them had questions while none had the answer.

Erish was watching all these discussions from the corner of the headmaster's cabin. The Headmaster saw Erish and then continued his discussions.

After much debate and discussions, Headmaster asked the teachers to leave.

'Erish! Come inside!' the headmaster requested.

Erish came to the headmaster's cabin. Unlike usually the headmaster was not seated on his chair but was resting on the sofa adjacent to his chair. He was bandaged at the head and the torso.

Erish came toward his headmaster. Headmaster gestured him to the seat beside him.

Erish silently sat beside him. For a couple of minutes, none of them spoke. Finally, Headmaster asked, 'Ask what you want to ask?'

'Who were they and where did they take away Asmi?' Erish asked.

'I don't know much about them. I was informed something like this would happen a long time ago. I waited and trained myself for yesterday and I failed.'

'How did you know something like this would happen?'

'For that, you need to know my past.' His headmaster replied.

'Your Past?' Erish asked.

'Yes! My past' Headmaster answered,' Come with me.' Saying so the headmaster took him into his past.

The headmaster walked himself up to the centre of his cabin. A mysterious symbol was at the centre of his cabin. It was the symbol with a Warrior holding a golden sword circumscribed inside a circle.

'By the powers vested in me. I command the gateway to open up.' The headmaster used a mantra.

No sooner was the mantra spoken that the very ground beneath Erish's feet began to move. A wide opening had emerged from the ground with staircases that led beneath the ground.

Erish had visited the headmaster's cabin countless times yet he never suspected that there was a hidden pathway beneath the cabin. Erish was nonplussed by the magic of this. He was unable to utter any words.

The Headmaster spoke up, 'Come quick. We need to save Asmi and the rest of them.' And the headmaster made his way through the stairs to whatever lay underground it.

Erish too followed suit.

The way was completely dark as Erish entered the underground stairs. Tiny insects were crawling alongside the walls of the stairs. The stairs were going round and round beneath the surface. The headmaster was leading the way to the other side. Erish tried keeping his pace with the headmaster.

At one stair he slipped his foot and lost his balance. He tried to maintain his balance by trying to find support from the adjacent walls but his twisted arm failed him. He tumbled from one stair to the next one when suddenly the headmaster caught him before he incurred much damage.

They reached the bottom of the stairs. It was a tiny room for a single person it was lit with candles and lamps. The whole place was like a hidden secret only to be revealed at the proper time.

At one end of the room was an ottoman. It was covered with old and ragged sheets. In front of the ottoman was a bookshelf filled with books, papers, and parchments. Strange symbols eclipsed the whole place. Bizarre objects were hanging from the rooftop.

The Headmaster slowly walked towards the ottoman. The light from the lamps and candles were casting back and forth shadows on his face. He seated himself on one side of the ottoman as memories came back flooding.

Erish was confounded by all the out of place objects found in the room. He looked at his headmaster who was half reclining towards the ottoman as if speaking to someone.

'People with selfish desires and evil intentions will one day come' the headmaster's father was speaking to him.

It was a long time since his father's health was not keeping well. The headmaster knew this day would soon come and waited in patience.

'My father took a promise from me to protect this school and whoever took shelter in his school. My father in turn made a promise to his father to safeguard the school and its refugees. All my life I kept my promise. Now it is your turn, my son, give me your promise.' The headmaster's father requested.

'Father!' the headmaster replied, 'I do promise. I will do whatever you want me to do!'

'My son, my father told me on his deathbed, that sooner or later people with selfish desire and evil intentions will come and try to realize the evil deeds you have to stop them.'

The headmaster held his dying father's hand as his father continued, ' I have taught you tantric mantra's. Promise me, son, that when the time comes you will protect this school and whosoever is sheltered in it.'

'I promise, father!' the headmaster promised, 'I promise that whenever the time comes I will protect the school and whosoever is sheltered in it!'

His father ran a hand over the headmaster's head in an affectionate manner. His father looked at him, his eyes were moist. He said, 'I know you would!' and smiled. Suddenly his hand fell.

The headmaster grasped his father's hand which was now lifeless. Just like that, his father departed forever.

Erish saw that his headmaster was in pain over something that happened in this room. He didn't know what to do but his empathy told him to go console his headmaster.

He walked up to his headmaster and placed a consoling hand over his fingers.

The headmaster came back from his reverie. He looked at Erish.

'This was the very place where I last talked to my father. He was everything for me. I lost my mother very early from that moment onwards my father filled the role of my mother as well. He asked me for a promise. I made him a promise that whenever the time comes I will protect the school and its children from whatever disaster it will befall. And today I failed to keep my promise' The headmaster said in a very painful voice, 'I failed to protect my school children.'

Erish asked, 'You knew something like this would happen?'

'No!' the headmaster replied, 'I only knew something would happen but what happened today was beyond my comprehension.'

'What was it that your father told you?'

'He told me that people with selfish desires and evil intentions would someday come to cause harm to innocent and helpless people.'

' Please save Asmi!' Erish pleaded to the headmaster.

The headmaster sighed in helplessness, 'I tried. And I failed!'

'Then who will protect Asmi?'

'I don't know.'

'If you cannot protect her. Can we take someone else's help who could protect Asmi?'

'There is no one in this world who could protect Asmi from that monster. I was no match for him. He was stronger and more powerful than all of the people I know.'

'So, no one can save Asmi?!' Erish asked in a tearful voice.

'I am afraid' the headmaster replied in a defeated voice, ' there is no one who can save your sister.'

'But there must be SOMEONE who can?' Erish protested.

The last words Erish spoke brought life to the headmaster. Suddenly hope swells up in the headmaster's heart. Now he had a faint hope that perhaps not all was over. Yes, he might have failed from preventing the school children from being abducted by those outsiders but he did not fail. The outsider mentioned that he would have them sacrifice in a fortnight that means there may still be some time some hope to summon the one who can.

'THE ONE WHO CAN!' Headmaster repeated Erish's last words. 'There is someone who can save your sister!' said the headmaster in a voice full of hope and enthusiasm.

'Who?!' Erish questioned with hope in his voice.

The headmaster stood up to his full posture. He looked directly at the candle flames that were swinging back and forth. The reflection of the flames was intensified in his eyes.

He answered with might, 'THE WARRIOR BORN FROM THE FLAMES OF FIRE!'

Erish was silent at those words.

The headmaster turned to Erish looked straight into his eyes and said, 'THE ONE WHOSE NAME IS: THE GOLDEN WARRIOR!'

CHAPTER 5

Giriraj was deep in meditation. He was powerfully built with strong muscles and a fine-tuned body with a long growing black beard. If someone saw him they would not suspect how old he was! To all appearances, he was only fifty years old. He wore a simple white dress before the burning candles deep in contemplation.

He was searching for the solution to the impending disaster he helped to create. He was seeking redemption on how to correct his wrong. He tried previously and he failed. This would be the last time if he failed this time it will all be over.

His students were practicing fighting with each other. The teachers were declaring out the mistakes committed by the students and started hectoring them to improve their performance.

All of them were busy in their respective duties when someone gave them an unexpected visit.

The huge eagle landed in the middle of the fighting ground followed by other frighteningly large birds. The students and the teachers were nonplussed by the sudden appearance of these creatures on their training ground. They watched as people climbed themselves down from the huge birds.

Charvik stepped his foot on the holy fighting ground.

Giriraj who was deep in his meditation felt a storm approaching him. the air which was mild a few moments ago was now roaring. Giriraj knew that Charvik had come.

He opened his eyes only to find two black coal eyes staring back at him. he was the same boy who at one time was Giriraj's favourite student. Now that same boy filled him with remorse and anger.

'Hello, Master! ' Charvik spoke.

Giriraj saw around himself. All his teachers and students were held captive by Charvik's followers by a knife at their throats.

Giriraj had waited for 300 hundred years for this day, preparing himself to face his creation yet somehow he felt inadequate to the task.

'What happened, master? Will you not try to stop me now?' Charvik taunted him.

Giriraj held his patience. He knew if he lost his cool. Charvik would kill his students and teachers to just make him angrier. He had experienced it before.

'You will never succeed…' Giriraj tried to complete that sentence but could not.

'In your evil intentions?' Charvik asked his voice was cool. 'These were the same words you used before. And you know how that went. I cannot be stopped.'

Giriraj swallowed his pride. He tried stopping Charvik before but failed. He maintained a defeated silence.

'Come with me,' Charvik said.

Giriraj followed knowing if he refused to obey him he will kill his students and teachers.

They reached the centre of the sacred fighting ground.

'My evil intentions for the coming fortnight,' Charvik said as a matter-of-factly.

Giriraj was aghast and disgusted by the look of it. They were mere small school going, kids. They were tied down like scapegoats ready to be butchered. All of them were crying from fear and pain. Giriraj wanted to help those kids but he was helpless.

'Charvik stop this madness!' he pleaded.

'I will after this fortnight is over,' Charvik answered.

Giriraj knew that if Charvik succeeds this time it will all be over.

He looked at Charvik who was staring back into his eyes.

Charvik was enjoying the look of helplessness in his ex-master's eyes. How far had he truly come! There was once a time when Giriraj was the most powerful and formidable Tantric in the tantric world. He had been Charvik's inspiration from the beginning.

Charvik still remembered his childhood when he wanted to be one of the best tantrics in the world. He copied Giriraj in every way he could. He promised himself he would one day surpass his master and he did it too. That seemed like only yesterday when Charvik was asking Giriraj about how to increase the power of one's mantra and now here he was with the same man who at one time was the most powerful of their lot.

'I cannot be stopped,' Charvik said. ' If you want to try stopping me and failing for the final time. You know where to find me.'

Charvik and his followers left with their captured kids.

Giriraj fell to the ground on his knees as helplessness and memories came back flooded to him. His disciple came running towards him to lend him support.

Giriraj opened his eyes. Charvik was standing above him. He

was weakened by the fight. He failed in stopping Charvik from accomplishing his evil plans. Charvik stood there laughing with madness. He looked one final time at Giriraj and said, 'I cannot be stopped.'

'Master!' Giriraj's disciple said shaking Giriraj. Giriraj came back to his senses. He looked at the sky. He saw Charvik and his followers flying away with little children. Giriraj sighed in defeat.

'Who is the Golden Warrior?' Erish asked the Headmaster.

The Headmaster quickly darted towards the adjacent bookshelf before him. he started scanning books after books, pages after pages, letters after letters.

Erish saw his headmaster was desperately searching for something but what? He didn't know. The headmaster seemed to have forgotten or perhaps did not care about the injuries he suffered just a couple of hours ago against the Outsider.

He bent on his knees and started removing all the books from the shelves. There was a small box hidden behind the large old books.

Erish saw the small box. It was carved out of some old metal. It was rusting like it was placed there for ages. The thing that caught Erish's attention was the symbol carved out on the box. It was the same symbol he saw a while ago. It was the symbol of the Warrior holding the Golden sword circumscribed inside the circle.

The headmaster quickly found the old twisted key from the shelf and opened the box.

Erish went closer to take a look at what was inside the box. There was nothing inside the box.

The Headmaster then uttered a few mystic words, 'By the powers vested in me, I command you to reveal yourself.'

As soon as he uttered those words a bright golden glow emerged from the box so bright that for a brief moment everything turned to golden colour. The brightness was such that Erish had to close his eyes from too much light entering his eyes.

Little by little the golden rays dissolved into the room sparkling everywhere.

The Headmaster leaped his hand inside the box which contained a golden piece of paper. Something was scribbled on it.

The headmaster seated himself on the ottoman and looked at the golden piece of paper.

Erish came next to the headmaster and took a peek at the paper. A verse of the poem was written on it.

The headmaster recited the verse in a slow voice :

> The one who fears neither the God,
>
> Nor the devil,
>
> The One who fears neither the man,
>
> Nor the beast,
>
> He can be found by following the morning Star,
>
> He is the one named 'The Golden Warrior!'

Erish did not understand the meaning of the verse. His headmaster uttered, 'He can be found by following the morning Star, He is the one named the Golden warrior!'

'What is the meaning of it?' Erish asked.

'It means that to find the Golden Warrior we have to follow the morning star.' The headmaster answered.

'The morning star?' Erish quipped.

'The Sun', Headmaster answered, 'Sun is also referred to as the morning star.'

'Who is the Golden Warrior?'

'I don't know. My father had informed me that should I fail in protecting my school and its students, if the challenge before me is more powerful than I could ever be. If I cannot save my school and students for whatever reason I am supposed to go request the golden warrior to save my students from whatever disaster befell them.'

'Will you go and request the Golden warrior to save Asmi?'

'No, I cannot. I am too weak to do anything now. And in the present circumstances, no one else could either. We will require the teachers here to take care of the traumatized kids. But you can go Erish. I will arrange a carriage for you tomorrow early in the morning. You have to go looking for the golden warrior and then convince him, request him to save Asmi and all the other kids. We don't have much time. We only have a fortnight to save them. And the Golden Warrior is the only one who could defeat that Outsider. The Golden Warrior is our only hope.'

The headmaster looked affectionately at Erish and requested, 'Will you go?'

Erish answered, 'I will!'

CHAPTER 6

The Next day early in the morning the Headmaster arranged for the carriage as promised. Erish was prepared to leave. He packed his bag with essential commodities. The Headmaster gave him a small bag full of gold coins 'You will need this', he had said.

And so Erish left in the carriage. He had never left the school before. It was his home but for the first, he was going out into a world he knew little about. Inside the carriage, he hugged his bag, Asmi had sewed that bag for him. No matter how hard he would save his sister. He would find the mysterious Golden Warrior and take his help to save his sister.

He was well on his way in his quest for The Golden Warrior! Little did he knew then what all things lay before him.

The Headmaster saw as the carriage took off Erish in the direction of the Morning Star. He held hope against hope that perhaps Erish would find and convince the Golden Warrior on time.

He still had an important thing to do. He has to send a message to an important person that Erish was coming for the Golden warrior.

He went straight back into his chambers and wrote something on a piece of paper. He then dipped the piece of paper into a bowl full of water. He uttered, 'By the powers vested in me I command you to deliver the message.'

As soon as the words were out of his mouth. The water in the bowl started churning rapidly and the paper vanished in the water.

 Yajin helped Agathashatru in the direction of the Golden Chamber. As always Agathashatru stood there before the golden chamber. Yajin had experienced it before as well. Agathashatry would just keep looking at the large Golden Doors. A symbol was carved out on the doors: A warrior holding a golden sword circumscribed within a circle.

Yajin had heard about the legend of the Golden Warrior. The warrior born from the flames of fire. More powerful and formidable than any other tantric in the world. He only comes when he thinks it is important to come. Rest of the time he is in a deep slumber waiting to be woken up.

Yajin had never set his foot inside the golden chamber and he had heard that Agathashatru was the last man alive to set his foot inside the golden chamber.

Yajin has asked countless times to have a single visit inside the chamber, he was refused every time. After much perseverance, he was informed that to open the Golden Chambers he would require the Golden Key and that to summon the Golden Warrior he would require the Golden sword.

Agathashatru muttered to himself, 'When will you come, when will you wake up from your slumber.'

Yajin was aware of Agathashatru's mumblings. He simply did not understand him. There was plenty now for him to know about and to learn. He was a beginner in the tantric world and he had mastery to achieve in it.

He often wondered how would it be to meet the Golden warrior. Little did he knew his wish would come true soon, very soon.

The Old man in violet robes was seated in his small room. There was a bowl of water in front of him. He was resting against the wall when the water started spinning in the bowl. 'A message' he thought. He went to the bowl and dipped his hand in the water, he received a piece of paper. Something was scribbled upon it. He was not able to read the message on it.

He took the paper and laid it before the table in front of him. He muttered, 'By the powers vested in me, I command you to reveal me the message.'

As soon as he said it, a message was now visible on the piece of paper.

He read it: A boy is coming for the Golden Warrior.

The Old man sighed. He knew what it meant. 'Charvik had risen!'

The Old man's name was Hridyanshu.

Erish was on his way towards the dock at the Great Lake. His headmaster read the following on the backside of that golden piece of paper:

'Cross the Great Lake. In the Isle of Forrest will you find the one, the one whose name is The Golden Warrior!' A name was scribbled on it, Hridyanshu.

Accordingly, he arranged the carriage for Erish early in the morning. He also informed the carriage man to drop Erish at the dock of the Great Lake.

It had been a ride of more than two hours. Erish looked sideways at the window of the carriage it was moving through a thick forest.

Wild animals were making frightening noise. Erish hugged his bag closer.

'You seem to be tensed?' the carriage man asked looking backward at Erish.

'Ah!' Erish looked at the carriage man. He was a teenage boy with a handsome face. 'I don't know. I want to save my sister Asmi. And I don't know how to. And I don't know if the Golden Warrior will help me?'

'Help will always come to you', the carriage man gestured knocking with his hand, ' if you knock, the right doors.'

About an hour later, they reached the dock.

Erish got himself out of the carriage with his bag. The carriage boy left him after dropping him at the dockyard.

The wind was blowing fast near the dockyard. Erish looked around there were many ships anchored against the boarding line. This place unlike the forest was much crowded. A fisherman was arranging their fishes while the fisherwoman was selling the fishes to the customers.

Erish had to find the Ship that went to the Isle of Forrest. His headmaster informed him that he was to meet a person named Hridyanshu.

He walked up to the boarding line and watched as passengers were busy boarding ships.

One man was screaming like his life depended on it. 'Isle of flowers come to this side.'

Others were screaming too in competition. Erish listened with rapt attention to what all places were being called.

'Isle of Hot water pools'

'Isle of animals.'

'Isle of Fruits.'

'Isle of berries.'

...

But no one said, 'Isle of Forrest.'

Erish was scared of asking this big looking man who seemed to be too busy. Plucking up courage he went to a man who was screaming from a ladder, 'Isle of creepers! All come to this side!'

'Sir, do you know which ship we can board the isle of Forrest?'

The sound of the crewmen screaming for their respective locations and the crowd of passengers talking to themselves was loud enough that no person could hear each other.

Erish's voice was inaudible in that cacophony.

The man asked, 'where boy?'

Erish answered, 'Isle of Forrest!'

The man unable to hear asked once again, ' Where boy?!'

Erish answered with all his might, 'TO THE ISLE OF FORREST!'

This time the people all went silent. The entire dockyard was still and soundless as if no one was present there.

But people were present there. Erish could see the look of horror on their faces. Everyone was watching him or more aptly staring at him. Some women were gossiping about what they had just heard. Crewmen from other ships came forward to have a watch on who wanted to go to the Isle of Forrest. Small boats were rocking on the waves while their boatsmen kept staring at the boy who wanted to go to the Isle of Forrest.

Erish understood without mistaking that the Isle of Forrest was a foreboding place. A place where no one would likely venture.

The crewman to whom Erish told he wanted to go TO THE ISLE OF FORREST had a grim expression on his face.

He came down from the ladder and looked at Erish.

Erish was oblivious about what to do.

The crewman said, 'Boy! Go away! There is no such place as the Isle of Forrest.'

Erish knew he was lying. 'You don't understand I have to go to the Isle of Forrest.'

'I do understand. You don't have to go to the Isle of Forrest, You WANT to go to the Isle of Forrest.' Came the terse reply.

Erish said in a lowly voice, 'Yes! I WANT to go to The Isle of Forrest!'

'Well, boy. What is the reason you …'

People were crowding nearing them to hear their conversation. 'What the heck! Go from here! Mind your own business!' heckled the crewman to the nearby on comers. They went away at the sudden aggressive reproach.

People now gave the crewman and Erish their space to talk.

He continued, 'Well boy. You come with me!'

Erish continued walking behind the crewman. People were still whispering about them.

The Crewman led Erish to the end of the dockyard. There was a ship anchored at the edge of the dockyard board. This one was bigger and much stronger than the rest of them. It was made of strong and bulk wood. Crafted stylishly. Its name was displayed on the board hanging from the sides: Where Ever You Go.

Erish boarded the magnificent ship. There were a couple of crewmen working on ropes. Erish looked at them. There was a man with a strong built. His veins were visible from his body.

'What happened?' that man asked in a strong voice.

The Crewman who brought Erish to the ship informed him, ' Avyay, this boy wants to go to the Isle of Forrest!'

Immediately the crewmen on the ship who were busy with their ropes started staring at Erish.

Erish did not felt good by their looks upon him.

The sturdy built man, Avyay came walking towards Erish. He bent on his one knee to level himself with Erish's height and looked straight into his eyes.

Erish saw fierce determination and dedication. Those were fearless eyes. It was as if the man had seen so much in life that there was nothing in the wide wake world to scare him. There was a vivid scar on his face stretching from his left temple towards his right jaw.

'What makes you want to go to the Isle of Forrest boy?' he asked sternly.

'My sister was kidnapped by some outsiders. Only the Golden warrior can save her. I need to find the Golden warrior and request him for help!' Erish parroted the entire episode that had happened at the school and how his headmaster has sent him to find the Golden Warrior.

'To what length can you go for your sister?'

'To whatever length need be.'

'Why should I take you to the Isle of Forrest ?'

Erish promptly took the bag of gold coins and held it before him.

The man started to laugh at Erish's innocence. That bag of gold coins will not save you from the monsters ahead. And that bag of gold coins certainly will not help you with the Golden warrior!'

'You know the Golden Warrior?'

'Yes, I do.'

'Can you please take me to him?'

'I know the Golden warrior only as a legend. Have heard about it from someone.'

'My headmaster had told me to meet Mr. Hridyanshu. He is the Golden warrior. I have to meet him.'

'Lo behold! I know Mr. Hridyanshu!'

'You know him?!'

'Yes, I do. He happens to be someone close.'

'Can you please take me to the Isle of Forrest to meet the Golden Warrior?'

The man said, 'But before we go there, I want to know something boy?'

'What?' asked Erish slowly.

'If at all a time comes when you have to die for your sister are you willing to die?'

Erish was taken aback by that question. He didn't know how to counter it. The man was looking at him waiting for an answer.

That thought never occurred to Erish. He was wondering if he had to give his life to save his sister.

He looked at the man and said, 'Do I have to die?'

'Maybe yes. Maybe no. We cannot tell now. BUT,' Avyay tensed, ' if a moment comes when you have no choice but die for your sister: Will You Die?'

Erish looked straight into the man's eyes and answered, 'I will.'

Avyay nodded his head in agreement. 'Fine boy, then I will take you to the Isle of Forrest.'

The ship 'Where Ever You Go' thus left the dock and made its sail in the direction no other shipmen or crew dared to sail. They were going to the Isle of Forrest and Erish was eagerly waiting to meet the one whose name is The Golden Warrior!

CHAPTER 7

The Moon rose high on the horizon. The clouds formed mist around it. Wolves were howling at the look of it. Night birds were taking flight and there was a gentle shower of rain. The air smelt of soil.

Charvik took one deep breath of fresh air into his lungs. Experiencing the taste of being alive. He had waited for so long. How many obstacles did he not overcome to get where was now standing? His kin had ostracized him treated him like an outsider. But he was going to accomplish what he was meant to accomplish in a couple of days ahead. All of them tried to stop him and all of them failed.

A wicked smile came over Charvik's face at that thought.

Mahakethu walked in at that moment.

'You called for me?' Mahakethu asked.

'Yes, I did. 'Charvik replied, 'Make preparations for the first sacrifice. We will begin tonight!'

'As you say. I will instruct the others for the preparations. I will inform you once it is done.'

Mahakethu left Charvik alone in his room.

After Mahakethu left. Charvik stood at the window for some time looking at the sky, stars, and the moon. At least he was nearing his dreams.

Mahakethu went to the others and ordered, 'Charvik wants to start the sacrifices from tonight. Make the preparations for it. Quick.'

'You', Mahakethu said to one of them, 'Bring one of the sacrifices.'

As instructed, he went to bring one of the sacrifices.

Asmi was tied along with the other kids. None of them had fallen asleep. They were in severe trauma at what had happened to them. All of them were crying.

Asmi was tied her hands behind her back. Seated or rather thrown behind the bars. She was alone in her jail. She could hear the screams and cries of other kids. Her jail was at least a thousand years old the looks of it.

The outsiders had kidnapped and brought them to hear. As they were flying through the sky she saw that it was a huge castle lost in time.

Now from within, she could see spiders and cobwebs all around her room. There was little place for her there. She sat in a corner crying. She had such a sheltered life at the school. The headmaster and the teachers took such good care of her and now she was with these dreadful outsiders. She didn't know what were they planning to do with her but she knew whatever they were planning to do was not good for her.

She taught about her little brother Erish. How just yesterday had she tied him the Rakhi and promised to take care of him. How would Erish feel when he saw her in that situation? She tried to locate Erish earlier but failed. Perhaps he escaped the outsiders and saved himself. Or perhaps he was caught up and thrown into a prison-like her.

Her mind was thinking about a lot of things at once. What would her fate be? What are these Outsiders Intentions? What are they planning to do to her and these other kids?

She had no answer to any one of them.

As instructed by Mahakethu, he arrived at the prison rooms. They were dimly lit by the fire across lamps. His shadow was changing shapes by the sideways light coming from the lamps. The corridor of the prisons was long. He started walking from door to door. He saw the faces of the small kids all of them in fear. He smiled at the look of fear on their faces.

I had been with Charvik for all these years to achieve what he wanted and now after all these years I will finally get what I want, he thought.

He was scanning for the first sacrifice. He walked. He tried choosing a fat boy but then decided against it. None of them were appealing to his sense of choice. He walked through the corridor of prisons waiting for the perfect sacrifice.

At last, he found it. Or found her.

Mahakethu looked after the preparations. He also allowed the girl as the first sacrifice. He went to Charvik to inform him about it.

Charvik was seated in the long chair. Resting his back and arms on the chair. His head was fallen back and he seemed to rest a bit.

Mahakethu arrived. 'Charvik all is set.'

Charvik raised himself from the chair and said, 'Time to proceed.'

'Not yet.' Came the terse reply from someone unexpected.

The fire was consuming The Golden Warrior! His skin was melting in the heat of the fire. The pain was unbearable. He did not believe he could withstand the pain. As the fire was seething inside deeper and deeper burning every particle of his body. He screamed and roared in pain but it gave him little relief. The fire was doing its job. Then another wave of fire gushed into his body. He felt the fire going through his throat inside his body. The fire was reaching down into every atom of his body.

All around him people were chanting mystic mantras. He did not understand it.

With each passing moment, they increased the pace of their utterings, and with each uttering the wave of fire burst itself upon him. the fire was emancipating from their hands towards the Golden Warrior!

His life was slowly nearing its end. He tried to stay alive for a few more minutes but he not could endure the pain and fire anymore. Slowly his breathing began to slow down. His roar was dwindling little by little. He closed his eyes. The fire did not stop, it was still consuming him. In one last effort he screamed with whatever was left in him, 'STOP IT' but they did not stop, they could not stop, not now anyway. And then he died.

 Agathashatru woke with a start! He was covered in sweat. The sins of his past came back to haunt him now and then. He could still visualize him vividly while the fire was consuming him. While he screamed for help in pain when he roared to 'STOP IT' and yet Agathashatru roasted the man alive till he died.

Agathashatru was seated on edge of his sleeping bed. He was

disturbed by his past. He stood up and walked towards the mirror. He looked at the mirror and saw himself. His wrinkled face, his weary eyes, his scared soul all were visible to him.

Guilt was eating him. He looked pale like an old man. He signed in pain and defeat. He felt as low as he could. He tried stopping Charvik and failed. This would be the last time he will get a chance to stop him if he fails this time then all will be lost.

Keeping hope against hope he went to the Golden Chamber and struck there staring at the Golden chamber in the middle of the night.

He fell on his knees crying for strength and help before the great Golden chamber. The Golden warrior inscribed on the doors of the golden chamber was staring at him blankly.

The Moon was glaringly visible in the dead of the night. Erish had never seen the moon from the sea before. It felt so big and so near. Their ship hovered on the waves like a stick floating in the water.

Erish did not understand why everyone else at the dockyard was not ready to go to the Isle of Forrest. He was about to get an answer soon.

Inside the ship cabin, the crewmen sat singing songs and eating their food along with wine. Erish had his plate and ate it. There was an old man in the crew who just kept blankly looking at Erish. He spoke nothing but his silence was speaking volumes. He was thinking if they had done the right thing by agreeing to take Erish at the Isle of Forrest. But it was too late for regretting that decision now they had covered nearly half the distance already.

After his dinner, Erish went outside the cabin and started looking at the sea from the edge of the ship. He saw his reflection in the water. He smiled a big toothful smile and his reflection did the same. He looked also at the twisted arm of his hand it was looking shaky in the waves of the sea.

Just then he felt something was watching him from the depths of the sea. He couldn't make it out what it was but he felt large green eyes were looking at him through his reflection.

He focused on the green light coming from below. He tried to make sense of what it was. All the while the two green eyes were getting closer and closer to him. Erish bent a little bit to have a clearer picture of it amidst the wavering waves.

This time he saw a white light just beneath the green light. Getting closer and closer to him. Suddenly the speed of the bright green eyes and the white light were nearing him faster and faster and at last, he saw what it was.

It was a creature Erish had never seen before. He saw the creature's bright green eyes but what took his breath away was not the bright green eyes but the white light emerging beneath the green light. It was not a white light at all. It was the creature's humungous fangs that were reflecting the moon's light.

The Ship collided suddenly with something. Avyay was busy charting the course to the Isle of Forrest when the ship was dashed powerfully by something.

'What's happening there?' Avyay asked.

'It seems we are hit by something near the left side of the ship. 'One of his crewmen answered.

A scary thought rushed through Avyay's mind. Erish was alone on the left side of the ship. Without further thought, Avyay dashed to the left side of the ship.

Erish was dumbstruck by the creature approaching him from the depth of darkness inside the sea. He was immobilized in his position and the creature inched ever closer towards Erish.

The creature has been hungry for weeks. It saw its prey and ripped its way from the depth of the sea towards its prey. It came inches towards its prey and then opened his gigantic mouth its fangs fully exposed and lunged at Erish.

The fangs and jaws of the creature engulfed Erish from both the side. The creature's tongue was hissing for the taste of its prey. Erish's eyes widened at the jaws of the creature. And in one big bang, the creature chewed its prey.

The taste of metal was unsavoury to the creature. It spit the metal out of its mouth. Even after scaring its prey and lunging at it at a breakneck pace, it missed its mark.

The jaws of the creature missed Erish by inches. He was suddenly pulled back at the last moment when the creature had almost engulfed him in its jaws. Avyay had at the right moment seized him and pulled him back just before the creature's attack. Just in the nick of the time.

Avyay had met the creature before. It was one of these creatures that had given him his scar.

The Ship was being thrown from one side to another. Something big was attacking the ship from below. The crewmen all assembled at the edges of the ship. One of them screamed, 'What's happening?!'

Erish heard one of the crewmen answer it, 'Sea Dragons!'

All around the ship creatures started emerging from the sea.

These creatures were huge. They had the body of a serpent with wings attached to their bodies. They had meat-eating fangs. Two horns headed from their heads. The bright blue colour was reflecting on their skin. Their ears were large protruding outwards. Thorny pike scales were emerging around their bodies. Their eyes were dark orange. These creatures were licking the scent of their prey in the air with their tongues. Their tongues were bright purple. All of these creatures had a hungry look upon their faces.

In the dead of the night, the rain started pouring with all its might. The waves were crashing the ship from one direction to the other. The creatures started attacking the ship chewing whatever they could lay their mouths on.

'Grab for the Swords!'

One of the crewmen left running towards the basement to fetch the swords.

Avyay told Erish, 'You! Get to the basement quickly. The rest of the crew grab the swords and thrust them at the sea dragons' eyes and noses that send them back from where they came.'

As instructed by Avyay, Erish started running towards the basement. The clouds and the rain formed a dense fog all around the ship making it difficult to locate the way. The crewmen were struggling to defeat the sea dragons.

No one was monitoring the wheel of the ship and the ship was bending from one side to the other and the creatures dived at the ship for their prey. Crewmen were finding it difficult to hold their balance in the wreaking ship.

A sea dragon lunged at Avyay but Avyay ducked and thrust his sword in the creature's eyes. The creature howled in pain and went back scurrying from whatever depth it had come from.

'Keep thrusting at the eyes!' Crewmen were roaring to motivate their comrades.

Amidst this Pandemonium, Erish falling and getting up almost reached the stairs to the basement when something from the sea came up.

It was a big black sea dragon. Its eyes were black. Its tongue which was tasting the air for the scent was black. The scales were black. Its tooth was black. It was one big embodiment of black. It rose high and high above the sea curling its body. Water was shedding from its body as it was rising above the sea.

Another crewman who was observing the creature from the far side muttered in fear, 'King of Sea Dragons!'

A strong wave of sea waves crashed the ship from sideways. Erish fell losing his balance along with some other crewmen. A sword was sliding from the ship and came halting near Erish.

Avyay who was busy battling some other sea dragon heard someone yell at him, 'Avyay, the boy!'

Avyay jumped high in the air and threw his sword in the mouth of the sea dragon. The sea dragon tried chewing the sword. The sword sliced inside the creature's mouth and was dangling from the left side of the mouth of the creature. In pain, the creature retreated.

Avyay now looked at Erish. Erish was fallen on the deck. The big black sea dragon was preparing for its attack on Erish. Avyay glimpsed the Sword near Erish and shouted, 'Erish Quick, Pick the Sword!'

Erish was thunderstruck by the sight of the monster before him. He heard distant noises around him to get up. He heard the voice of Avyay shouting, 'Pick the Sword! Pick the Sword!'

He saw towards his left side; the sword was there. He saw in front of him, the sea dragon was looking at its prey.

Mustering up some strength he tried to get to the sword but somehow he felt weak, not up to the task. He didn't feel he could save himself from the monster.

Avyay was now running towards Erish. He was still shouting, 'Erish! Pick the Sword! And thrust it into the creature's mouth!'

Erish crawled towards the Sword. His twisted arm was jerking in fear. His heart was beating as fast as it could. Using his left hand, he caught hold of the sword but he was unable to pick it. The sword was too heavy for him.

Fear was overpowering Erish. He left the sword and saw the creature that had thrown itself at Him. He resigned in defeat. He could not save himself.

The creature opened its fangs and its tongue was jabbing outside surround Erish. That's when Avyay came rushing he picked the sword and with one strong chop sliced the monster's tongue freeing Erish from its clutches.

The monster howled in pain for some time. Its fury was rising and in anger, it dived at its assailant. Avyay was ready for it. In one stroke he delivered the sword at the hilt of the creature's mouth. The sword dug into the creature's mouth and emerged from above it. The creature languished for some time in pain. Throwing the ship from one side to the other. And died a slow death.

Erish was still in shock. It was too much for him. But he realized that he was saved.

Avyay was angry at Erish. He strode towards Erish and asked in an angry tone, 'Why did you not pick up the Sword?'

Erish tried to answer, 'I was scared. The Sword was too heavy for me. I only have one hand.' Erish gestured to his twisted right hand.

Avyay pulled Erish's left hand and spoke his voice was still angry, 'It doesn't matter how many hands you have got; what matters is what you have got in the one you have got.' He said pressing Erish's hand. 'These stupid sea dragons are nothing,' Avyay said kicking a dead sea dragon beside him, 'in front of what you will be facing coming ahead. And that time if you cry 'I have got only hand' YOU WILL DIE! If you fail to act at the decisive time then Your Sister Will Die! If you want to convince the Golden Warrior to come to your sister's rescue then having only one hand will be the least of your troubles.'

Erish was unaware of what he should say.

Avyay left him and went to steer the ship in the direction of the Isle of Forrest.

The night was nearing its end and the Sun was coming out from the horizon. The golden rays of the sun fell upon the ship. Avyay who was now steering the ship was the first on whom the rays fell. Erish saw it from the backwards and for one brief moment, he felt as if Avyay himself was the Golden Warrior.

Avyay caught Erish was watching him. He knew he was hard at Erish for not picking up the Sword. But it was for his own good. Still, he felt a tinge of guilt for his behaviour. He had hurt Erish too much.

He asked his crewmen to take charge of the steering wheel and strode towards Erish.

Erish was still upset by Avyay's scolding back then.

Avyay levelled himself at Erish's height and looked him straight in the eye. The rays of the sun fell upon him and gave him a golden aura. Avyay just kept looking at Erish. The wind was blowing near them. The wind ruffled Avyay's long hair. Then Avyay said with strictness, 'Erish! I going to tell you something which I want you to remember.'

Erish nodded his head in agreement.

Avyay continued, 'What I am going to tell you is very important for you, for your quest for the Golden Warrior, and in protecting your Sister's life.'

Erish muttered in a low voice, ' All right.'

Then Avyay muttered two words to Erish. Words Erish would never forget for the rest of his life.

CHAPTER 8

Aghori came forward holding a lantern in his hands. His eyes were crooked in different directions. The hand with which he was holding the lantern was also crooked. He had a long white beard. He was only in a saffron dhoti. His teeth were weakened with too much tobacco.

He interrupted, 'Not yet!'

Charvik and Mahakethu looked at the figure before them.

Both of them were surprised.

'Aghori?!' Charvik muttered.

'Yes!' Aghori replied with amusement in his eyes.

'How come you are here?'

'Don't ask unimportant questions Charvik.' Aghori continues, 'something is going on you should be aware of!'

Charvik got up from his chair and came face to face with Aghori, 'What?'

'There is this little boy with a twisted arm…' Aghori fetched a bowl of water and place it on the table beside him. he then opened a pouch bag that was hanging from his waist and took some black powder from it. He mingled the powder into the bowl of water and uttered, 'By the powers vested in me I command you to reveal me the boy with the twisted arm'

As soon as Aghori said those words, the water in the bowl started churning and an image was appearing in the bowl of water.

Charvik came closer to the bowl of water to see the image that was forming. He saw a boy with the twisted arm, the same boy with the twisted arm, the boy was talking to someone about something.

The boy was talking to the same old man who tried to stop Charvik at the school. The old man was telling the boy about how he can protect his sister from the outsiders. The old man told the boy about the only one who can save the boy's sister. The old man informed the boy about the Golden warrior!

Memories came back in Charvik's mind. The Golden warrior! The warrior born from the flames of fire.

Charvik whispered with contempt, 'The Golden Warrior...'

The image in the bowl now changed. The boy was now on his way to find the Golden Warrior. The boy was on a ship fighting sea dragons. In search of the Golden warrior...

'What is the meaning of it?' Mahakethu who was silent till now asked.

Aghori took a deep breath and answered, 'If the boy succeeds in finding the Golden Warrior then you all are doomed.'

Charvik countered, 'So many tried to find the Golden Warrior! No one succeeded. It's a myth.'

'Or so you think.' Aghori countered.

'Should we kill the boy?!' Mahakethu asked.

Charvik looked at Aghori. Aghori kept staring into Charvik's eyes.

'Wherever You Go!' was sailing along the coast of the isle of

Forrest. Erish stood on the deck and kept staring at the Island before him.

The Isle of Forest was densely covered with trees. The greenish colour was even darker and deeper than it was outside the Isle. Tiny insects and creatures were crawling in and around the bushes. Waves were softly crashing at the coast.

Wherever you halted at the sand coast before them. Avyay, Erish, and the crewmen stepped from the ship.

There was a tiny cottage right up on the mountain top on the Isle of Forrest. And a figure was looming there holding a stick for support covered in violet robes. Staring right at the people who descended from the ship.

Hridyanshu had been waiting eagerly since he received the message. He knew time is of the essence. Things must be done quietly and quickly.

Avyay and Erish started making their way towards the cottage while the rest of his crew remained at the coast with the ship.

Erish was still thinking of the two words Avyay had told him earlier this morning. The words still played in his head. Erish witnessed first-hand how courageous Avyay was. He wished if he could be like him. After all, Avyay was strongly built while Erish had a twisted arm.

In some time, they reached the cottage while the old man was eagerly awaiting their arrival. The old man jitterily came striding towards them. The Old man leaped towards Erish catching hold of his hand, he led him inside his cottage. Avyay followed them.

Erish could feel that the Old Man's cottage somehow felt familiar but he did not pay much attention to it. He was keen to save his sister Asmi from whatever fate befell her.

Erish asked out of breath at having to climb the mountain, 'Are you the Golden warrior?' his voice full of hope.

Hridyanshu negated, 'No boy, but I know someone who is.'

'Who is that someone?' Erish asked in desperation.

Hridyanshu quickly went to the shelves that were holding some ancient papers and brought back a piece of paper.

A verse was written on that piece of paper:

He's got the hands; to hold the sword,

He's got the will; to reach the goal,

He's got the feet; to scale the see,

He's got the strength; to reach the peak,

He can be found by crossing the mount,

He's the one named 'The Golden Warrior!'

Hridyanshu recited the verse mentioned in the piece of paper. He then turned the paper and a name was written on it: Indranuj.

'What is the meaning of it?' Erish asked.

'Beyond this jungle!' Hridyanshu continued, 'there is a mountain so big and so tall that it reaches the skies. On top of that mountain will you find the one whose name is the Golden Warrior!'

After a prolonged pause, he continued, 'But to get there you need to scale the mountain, and in the density of that mountain there lies a monster. A monster is so immense that whoever crossed its path did not return alive. You need to escape that monster and reach the top of the mountain. An almost impossible task. You have very little time kid; you need to get there and get there fast.'

'What is that monster Avyay asked?'

Hridyanshu looked at Avyay, 'Asin it's called. It is a giant humanoid except for the only thing it feeds on is human flesh.'

How Hridyanshu uttered the last sentence made an unsettling impact on Avyay. A flesh-eating humanoid. Never in his entire adventurous life did Avyay faced a flesh-eating humanoid.

He looked at the tiny Erish who was still trying to comprehend what sort of monster he had to deal with. Fear was evident in Erish's face.

Avyay knew if he let the boy go there alone he will never return.

Out of concern for Erish, Avyay said, 'In that case, I will accompany the boy in crossing the mountain.'

Hridyanshu replied in an undercutting voice, 'The boy must go alone!'

Avyay argued, 'But you said no one who met the monster came out alive.'

'Did I?' Hridyanshu asked, 'Well some did come back in corpses. But the boy wants to go to The Golden Warrior. And the Golden Warrior does not meet cowards. He only meets the valorous and courageous if you go in a herd he will never entertain you. I must repeat the boy must go alone.'

Avyay was in flux he did not know what to do?

Hridyanshu though approached Erish and asked, 'Will you go alone atop of the mountain outwitting and outsmarting the monster?'

Erish maintained a stunned silence.

Hridyanshu said, 'For your sister?'

Erish unassured of himself answered hesitatingly, 'I will.'

 'Let me go!' Asmi screamed and screeched at the outsider's hand who was forcibly dragging Asmi.

'You are not going to go anywhere. The only place you will be going is the sacrificial scapegoat!' the outsider replied with derisive laughter.

He dragged and dragged Asmi till they reached the sacrificial altar. It was a big mass of land surrounded by lava from all sides. Only one tiny bridge connected that landmass to the other side. Asmi saw the lava from the sides. It was boiling heat. The red colour lava was burning a boiling erupting various gas around the sacrificial altar.

The rest of the outsiders was creating some elaborate form of design in the centre of it. There was a Satan's symbol in the centre of it.

The outsider pushed Asmi in the centre of the design. Another outsider caught her and tied her up on the wooden plank such that her head was down on the plank.

Asmi was scared for her life. She knew what was coming to her.

She opened her eyes and saw the outsiders had rounded her up near the design in one peculiar pattern and they all started reciting some mantras.

Asmi tried to make sense of what they were doing. She observed from side to side and someone caught her eyes.

This was a giant Outsider who was smiling eerily at her. And then he drew the big black chopper and pointed towards it.

Asmi understood she was about to be slaughtered in some time.

The sounding of the reciting mantra was growing louder and louder. Their pace was increasing faster and faster. And now all of them were muttering in chorus.

Just then, Mahakethu arrived walking in long strides along with Aghori.

They stood near the design watching Asmi. And a moment later Mahakethu ordered, 'Finish her off!'

The Outsider with the big black chopper neared Asmi. He raised his chopper.

Asmi could feel the shadow of the outsider over her. Her eyes widen with fear and she started to cry for help. But there was no one to save her.

The Outsider brought down the big black chopper with a great 'THUD'.

Hridyanshu gave a map to Erish to manoeuvre the jungle. Avyay had one last talk with Erish before allowing him to go on his quest for the Golden Warrior.

Avyay drew his sword from his scabbard. The sword was glittering in the rays of the sun. He held it in front of Erish and asked him to take it.

'You will need it now more than ever in your quest to save your sister.'

Erish took the sword. He tried to manage the weight of his sword on his hand. It was a little heavy for him but Erish held it firmly nonetheless.

Hridyanshu said, 'All right Kid! Now go, Save your sister.'

Once again, Erish left for the mountains in his search for the one, the one whose name is the Golden Warrior.

CHAPTER 9

Afer Erish left for the mountains, Avyay asked Hridyanshu, 'Will the boy be safe out there?'

Hridyanshu nodded his head gesturing, 'No'

'Will the boy be able to save his sister?'

'I don't know. We will have to wait and see.'

'Then Why did you not allowed me to go with him, father?!' Avyay asked in fury.

'Because that would defeat the boy's purpose. Only the strong-willed would be able to summon the Golden Warrior. The weak-willed have no place for him.' Hridyanshu answered.

Avyay resigned in helplessness.

Hridyanshu walked rapidly into his cottage.

Avyay asked, 'What are you doing now?'

Hridyanshu answered, 'I have to inform somebody that the boy is coming for the Golden Warrior!'

Saying that Hridyanshu teetered into his cottage. He took a piece of paper scribbled a line on it and held the paper in the moving wind.

The paper vanished in the wind.

Hridyanshu knew it would be delivered to the right person.

'CLANG!' The sound was reverberating at the sacrificial altar.

The Outsider had deliberately missed his mark Asmi by the skin of her teeth.

Charvik had appeared just a moment ago and he had gestured him not to complete the sacrifice.

Mahakethu and Aghori along with the others saw as Charvik came striding towards the girl. His long figure was making even longer shadows. Shadows that could see through their dark red eyes.

'What happened?' Mahakethu asked.

'I just remembered that the boy with the twisted arm must be this girl's brother' Charvik continued, ' I recognize it now. He was trying to save this girl at school. And now that same boy is in the quest to save her by summoning the Golden Warrior. I want to kill her before his eyes. To make him watch all his efforts go in vain. To feel the pain of not able to protect his sister. Save her for later.'

Asmi had overheard their conversation. She was petrified with fear. Tears were still fresh in her eyes. She could feel Charvik approaching her. His long shadow fell over her and sent ripples of angst within her. She could not feel anything but pain and fear. Everything went dark and kept getting darker and darker. It was as if she was falling from a cliff trying hard to cling to some nearby support but nothing was there to support her. She felt getting being absorbed in a big black hole never to return. She screamed in fear but no one was there to hear her scream. Her skin started to burn with cold. The coldness was burning her skin her vision was getting blurred. She wished to come out of that dark hole.

Charvik caught her by her hair and said, 'How was the feeling being inside my inner hell?'

Asmi opened her eyes to saw the dark red eyes of Charvik and at once recognized that he was not a man but something beyond.

Charvik spoke, 'It seems your twisted brother is trying to save you. I will keep you alive. I will butcher your brother in front of your eyes. And then I will sacrifice you for the Final ritual.'

Asmi was too scared to say anything.

Charvik instructed one of the Outsiders to take her back to the prison.

Erish started crossing the mountain. It was all covered in Forrest. He was all alone with nothing but the sword that Avyay gave him and the bag that contained some of his stuff.

The Forrest was dark and scary. Erish was intimidated by the unknown atmosphere. Slowly mustering up courage he started scaling the mountain. He looked above at the height of the mountain. The mountain seemed big, mighty, formidable, and scary.

He started climbing up. He held on to the rocks with his single left hand. The mountain was difficult to climb for two-handed people but Erish somehow managed even with a single hand. The Dust was flying in his eyes, he almost lost his balance. Still struggling and balancing he kept on going forward. He looked below and then above to see how much distance he covered and how much distance remained. Every time he scaled considerable distance he looked above only to find the mountain did not diminish at all if at all it seemed to grow even bigger.

Unknown insects met him on his way making sounds he had never heard before. At one point he was exhausted, he found some small place to take some rest. He's been scaling the mountain for so long and yet he did not reach the top.

There was an eerie silence around him as if despair and hopelessness were asking him to return. Erish held on once again scaling the scary mountain. His bag and the sword which Avyay gave him were making his journey even more difficult. The sword was too weighty for him.

At intervals, the thought of the humanoid Asin also haunted him. So far he had managed not to encounter the Asin. It was better to simply scale the mountain rather than coming into contact with the Asin. He was too tired if he encounters the Asin then his legs would fail him for sure. There was acute pain in his legs from scaling. He got bruises and cuts around his hands and legs.

When he was pulling himself up from a shelf in the mountain all his weight and the weight of his bag and the sword was lifted by his sole hand. His twisted arm was of no use to him. He felt his shoulder would dislocate if he would pull himself like that. With all the pain and exhaustion Erish still ploughed ahead.

Asmi was back in her cell. It took several hours for her to recover from the trauma she endured just a few hours ago. She sat there traumatized. She was thinking of what Charvik had told her. 'It seems your twisted brother is trying to save you.' Erish was trying to save her. It gave her some hope but then she recalled what Charvik had told her later. 'I will butcher your brother in front of your eyes.' She feared for the life of her brother Erish.

Whatever these Outsiders were and whatever especially Charvik was, these were not normal people they were dangerous. There was no way of knowing how Erish was trying to save her. Even if Erish tried he would fall into the clutches of these Outsiders and he will be killed.

She remembered the sacrificial altar. That Sacrificial Altar was the place where she would be butchered along with the rest of the kids. She remembered how those Outsiders were reciting some mantras in unison. How the whole affair was otherworldly.

She recollected that when they were reciting the mantras something was happening there. Black Dark aura was emerging from that sinister place. All of the Outsiders were twinkling in black little stars. Their sound was still reverberating in her ears.

She felt how it was when Charvik's shadow had fallen over her. It took her to some cruel hellish place. It was unsettling for her. Her mind was shifting gears from one thought to the other. She did not know what tomorrow would bring her.

She knew she had little time left. Her last hope being Erish.

Erish reached a plain spot to take some rest. He has scaled a considerable amount. The sight was plain before him. After taking his breather, he tried going over. He noticed that the trees were less here.

Before him was a giant cave. 'Surely this must be the way to go' Erish thought.

Erish came close to the giant cave. Just then sinister laughter emerged from the surroundings. The laughter was growing louder and louder, coming closer and closer. Erish tried to locate where the laughter was coming from? He saw from left to right but no one could be seen.

The ground beneath him started shaking. He could hear the Stomping! The sound coming near him. But from where?

It seemed he was surrounded by all over. The maniacal laughter was echoing from the mountains.

Erish focused on the greenish bushes to his left side. Something was coming close. The trees and bushes started shaking wildly and the laughter was moving ever closer.

And then the thing came out from the giant trees. It was Asin. Hridyanshu had warned Erish about the Asin.

It was a giant humanoid. With Wolff like teeth. It had horns on its head. Its skin was marred in red colour. Its eyes were bulging big and the Asin was sniffing in the air with his large nose. Its eyes were hungry for human flesh.

The Asin looked at Erish and started his evil laugh. Fear gripped Erish. He had never encountered such a monster before. He was no match for this monster.

The Asin aimed at Erish with his hand. But Erish quickly controlled himself and dashed to his right side. To one side of him was the edge of the cliff. He could not go back. He hand to climb that cliff up. With Asin at his heels he could not go down he had to run and run.

The Asin started chasing Erish. Its large legs trying to crush down Erish. Erish almost came under its feet twice.

Erish ran with all his might to dodge the Asin.

The Asin came closer to Erish and tried to pick Erish in its hand.

It was not able to capture Erish but dashed him to the corner of the mountain wall.

Erish was trapped now. He was cornered against the mountain wall and the Asin was staring right at Him.

He lunged for Erish.

Erish just then spotted a small opening in the mountain wall and scurried into it like a rat escaping a cat.

The Asin wriggled his fingers into the small hole trying to reach Erish. Erish went deeper and farther into the hole. The Asin's finger was just a meter away from him. The Asin was not able to reach him.

Finally, Erish fell. His lungs were demanding more air. His body outran his capabilities. Erish sat there looking out at the Opening.

Asin was still there. Erish could see the giant was peeping into the hole staring at its dinner.

Fear gripped him. His hands were shaking. He looked at his twisted arm, the Rakhi Asmi tied him was on his twisted arm. He remembered the day in school when Asmi tied him the Rakhi and what it meant. The Headmaster had explained to him that Rakhi was a symbol of a brother protecting his sister. He started the quest in the first place to save his sister but now his own life was in danger. He didn't know what to do. There was no one to help him essentially all on his own. He felt weak not up to the task. He felt hopeless. He sat there in a corner clutching his bag trying to control his fear. Something Hard felt in his bag. He opened his bag and it contained the Sword Avyay gave him.

Erish picked the sword and held it. The sword was hard as Iron.

Memories came back to him:

Avyay was angry at Erish. He strode towards Erish and asked in an angry tone, 'Why did you not pick up the Sword?'

Erish tried to answer, 'I was scared. The Sword was too heavy for me. I only have one hand.' Erish gestured to his twisted right hand.

Avyay pulled Erish's left hand and spoke his voice was still angry, 'It doesn't matter how many hands you have got; what matters is what you have got in the one you have got.' He said pressing Erish's hand. 'These stupid sea dragons are nothing,' Avyay said kicking a dead sea dragon beside him, 'in front of what you will be facing coming ahead. And that time if you cry 'I have got only hand' YOU WILL DIE! If you fail to act at the decisive time then Your Sister Will Die! If you want to convince the Golden Warrior to come to your sister rescue then having only one hand will be the least of your troubles.'

Avyay levelled himself at Erish's height and looked him straight in the eye. The rays of the sun fell upon him and gave him a golden aura. Avyay just kept looking at Erish. The wind was blowing near them. The wind ruffled Avyay's long hair. Then Avyay said with strictness, 'Erish! I going to tell you something which I want you to remember.'

Erish nodded his head in agreement.

Avyay continued, 'What I am going to tell you is very important for you, for your quest for the Golden Warrior, and in protecting your Sister's life.'

Erish muttered in a low voice, ' All right.'

Then Avyay muttered two words to Erish. Words Erish would never forget for the rest of his life.

Avyay drew his sword from his scabbard. The sword was glittering in the rays of the sun. He held it in front of Erish and asked him to take it.

'You will need it now more than ever in your quest to save your sister.'

Erish remembered the words Avyay told him. It gave him courage. He stood up.

A few drops of water fell on his head. He looked above there was light coming from above. There was a small opening above.

Erish removed the Map Hridyanshu gave him earlier. He looked at the map. It was directed in the map of the giant cave apparently the Asin's cave was the only way to get to the other side of the mountain. For that, he needs to outwit the Asin.

Something came dashing at Erish. It was a sharp-pointed metal spear! The Asin was now trying to spear in his weapon to catch Erish.

Erish knew he did not have much time. The Asin would catch him in some time one way or the other.

He looked at his surrounding there where some creepers hanging from above the ceiling. He could climb up with those dangling creepers.

He held the sword between his teeth tightly and started climbing the creepers with his one hand. Meanwhile, Asin continued its attempt to catch Erish.

Normally Erish would have been tired but not today not now. Even with one hand, he was climbing the creepers with the heavy sword between his teeth. He climbed the creepers and reached above.

The Asin was unaware that Erish has reached above that cave.

Erish came to the edge of the cave, he saw Asin was still absorbed in the small opening.

Erish held the sword in his hand firmly. The sword gave him strength.

Erish went a couple of steps back and came running with all his might and then he jumped off the edge.

Erish roared at the Asin. The Asin now looked above. The rays of the sun outlined the figure of Erish jumping right at him. Something was shining in his Hand: The Sword Avyay gave him.

The Asin opened his mouth wide open so that it can eat Erish in one gulp.

Erish was in mid-air the sword shining brightly in his hand and the Asin below his mouth wide open.

CHAPTER 10

Indranuj was enjoying a cup of tea sitting in his small house before the fire. Suddenly a breeze of wind ruffled his air.

'A message?' he thought.

He held his hand in the breezing wind and muttered, 'By powers vested in me. I command you to reveal yourself.'

A piece of paper appeared from the wind and Indranuj caught it.

As expected it was a message. A line was scribbled on it.

It read: Somebody is coming for the one whose name is The Golden Warrior!

Indranuj was deeply aware of what it meant. Another unfortunate fellow was after another nearly futile quest.

He was curious to know who this fellow was. He walked out of his small house.

Sun was above his head. He kept walking for some distance till he reached the end.

He was standing on the edge, on the precipice of the great mountain. He saw bellow as far as his eye could see their dark forest beneath it. He sighed. He wondered, 'Whoever is coming here they have passed through the Asin and the only handful of people were lucky enough to escape him while nearly all ended up dead.

He had too much hope at some time in his life but he now turned into a cynic believing life is not in one's hand.

Yet he held hope against hope in his heart perhaps this time it would be different.

Shwetakethu came striding towards Agathashatru along the long hall.

Yajin was seated with Agathashatru helping him with some herbal plants. He saw Shwetakethu approaching them with seriousness on his face. 'Something must be happening' Yajin thought. He was not able to comprehend the behaviour of his Masters from the past few days.

All of them were hurried as if time was low and something bad was about to happen. He asked Jatasya once about it, 'Why is everyone so worried?'

'The moment why Agathashatru is still alive from a thousand years is approaching.' Jatasya said, ' Our Master Agathashatru has failed previously. This is his last chance to stop the destruction he helped to create. If he fails this time all will be lost.'

Yajin still thought about it. He knew Agathshatru had outlived his time but why? He also knows that to outlive one's time one had to make others pay the price for it by their time. A horrifying thought came to him. He wondered if that was true?!

Shwethakethu reached them, 'Master I have a message from Giriraj?'

'From Giriraj! What is it?' Agathashatru asked.

'He said Charvik has returned and is preparing for the final rituals. He also captured the sacrifices for the final rituals. Time is getting out of our hands.'

Agathashatru got up on his trembling legs. 'So Charvik came back! It means this will be the last time I have to make good for the sin I committed.'

Everyone maintained a still silence except the Owl Onik.

'We will need the Golden Warrior to stop Charvik!' Agathashatru continued, 'We have to summon him soon.'

'But how? All the previous attempts went in futile. And even Giriraj has refused from summoning the Golden Warrior after the failed attempts. He holds the Golden Key for the Golden Chamber without the key and the Golden Sword there is no hope of the Golden Warrior!' Shwetakethu asked.

Just then Jatasya too came striding from the hall. He spoke, 'I got a message: Somebody was coming for the Golden warrior!'

'Who?' Shwethakethu questioned.

'I don't know. I got this message from Indranuj.' Jatasya answered.

Agathashatru was now contemplating the meaning of all these. The Puzzles were fitting together. He asked, 'Who did Indranuj say was coming?'

'Somebody was coming for the Golden warrior!' Jatasya showed him the message.

Agathashatru muttered holding the piece of the message in his hands, 'You read it wrong. It is not 'Somebody was coming for the Golden warrior!' it reads, 'Some boy was coming for the Golden warrior!'

Shwethaketu was surprised, 'A boy?!'

Agathashatru affirmed, 'Yes, a boy!'

Erish was hovering in mid-air. He held the sword tightly in his hand. He saw below the Asin had his mouth wide open.

Erish aimed at the Asin's eye and dived right at his mark.

He landed on the Asin's cheekbone and the sword pierced the Asin's left eye.

Pain seared in the Asin's eye. He blinked his eyes to remove the sword but the sword was digging deeper with each blink.

Erish after thrusting the sword in the Asin's eyes fell rolling, trying to clutch whatever he could of the Asin's body. The Asin was moving back and forth in pain. Erish fell to the ground.

His body absorbed the shock of the fall.

He saw upwards at the Asin. The act went as per his plan. The Asin was nearing the edge of the cliff.

Just one step and the Asin would fell off the cliff.

The Asin was still struggling with the sword in his eye.

Erish got up he saw that the Asin was at the edge.

He made a run towards Asin and gave one final push with all his might.

The Asin slipped off the cliff. And fell into the dark depths of the jungle below never to return.

Erish could hear the fearful cry of the Asin as it fell off.

Erish went to the edge of the cliff from where the Asin fell. He sat there staring below. He felt inexpressible emotions surging within him. He was shaken and was sweating profusely but he felt another emotion that was courage.

He looked above at the remaining mountain that he had to climb. It was still dense and it was getting dark as the sun was setting down.

Erish knew he needs to climb above but the once formidable, scary, and mighty mountain did not seem so formidable, scary, and mighty after all.

Erish did not know that he was being watched by different people sitting at different locations united by a single goal.

His Headmaster was looking at him through a bowl of water.

Hridyanshu was watching at him through a breeze of wind.

Indranuj was watching him through a stream of the river.

Erish neared the mountain peak. The peak was perpendicular to the ground. Erish balanced himself on the rocks. He stepped very carefully one slip and he would join the Asin below. Struggling against the rocks with one arm he pulled himself higher. He held the edge with one hand and forced himself higher to climb and get on the other side of the mountain.

Just then his fingers lost the grip and he fell.

But another hand caught him in the nick of the time. It was Indranuj.

Indranuj was keeping an eye on Erish ever since he got that message that he was coming for the Golden Warrior.

He was impressed by Erish's perseverance.

Pulling Erish higher he helped him to cross the edge and come over. Erish was bathed in dust and mud. There were bruises around his hands and faces.

Erish's heart was leaping fast. He almost lost his balance at the edge. Erish looked at the man who helped him. Instinctively, he knew that this was the man he was supposed to meet.

Indranuj asked Erish to follow him to his cottage. Erish followed.

The cottage was similar to the one at Hridyanshu.

Erish asked, 'Are you the Golden Warrior?'

Indranuj answered, 'No Kid. I am not the Golden Warrior. But I know someone who is The Golden warrior.'

Erish asked, 'Who is he? Where to find him? My sister is in danger. I need the Golden Warrior's help.'

Indranuj promptly removed a piece of paper from his robes and gave it to Erish. Indranuj had rummaged his old shelves to locate that paper as soon as he got the news that Erish was coming for the Golden Warrior.

Erish took the paper.

A verse was written on it:

<blockquote>

The one who fears neither the day

Nor the night,

The one who fears neither the sky

Nor the storm,

He's the one holding the Golden Sword,

He can be found by crossing the

Seven seas,

He's the one named 'The Golden Warrior!'

</blockquote>

Erish read the verse and looked up at Indranuj. Questions were looming in his head.

Indranuj looked at the quizzical face of Erish and understood the boy had questions in his mind.

Indranuj gestured Erish to sit down on his old chair and started his explanation:

'The one who took your sister. His name is Charvik. More than 1000 years ago…'

Yajin asked to find more about what was happening, 'Master! What's happening?'

Aghathashatru answered, 'More than a thousand years ago, I committed a sin I ought not to commit.'

There was a grim silence throughout. Yajin, Jatsya, and Shwethaketu all remained silent.

'The Tantrics were prospering. We were sharing our wisdom with lesser unfortunate folks. And one day this boy came to us requesting to teach him tantrism. My Master at that time had instructed me to teach Tantrism to everyone who came looking for it. And so, I started schooling the boy about tantrics and tantrism.

 The boy learned fast. He was more eager than ever to learn more. So, I thought him more. The boy's name was Charvik.

One day in our ancient library, the section of Dark Tantrism where no one was allowed to go was breached by Charvik. He stole a book from it: Beyond Life and Death. The book was written by Ipsit our most powerful tantric to date. Ipsit had mentioned in his book how one can prolong one's life and immortalize oneself. But to do so would require one to sacrifice others: The Sacrificial Ritual. If you sacrificed more than 1000 kids in one go by following the ritual mentioned in the book.

Charvik was very charismatic. He soon convinced the other boys about going beyond life and death. Of course, not all of them were convinced. Charvik along with the boys he managed to convince started kidnapping little kids from the village to mount the sacrifice. He needed 1000 kids so he started kidnapping from other villages as well.

The news soon reached us that some kids were disappearing from the villages and that the tantrics were doing it. Our Headmaster undertook a stern investigation into the matter. We were informed by the boys who had heard about the sacrificial ritual from Charvik. The Headmaster called for Charvik and the other boys and enquired about it.

Charvik was barely able to convince the Headmaster it was not his doing. The headmaster kept strict notice of his actions.

Finding out that he was the prime suspect, Charvik restricted his actions. He knew his veil will be lifted soon. So, he hurried up the preparations for the Sacrificial Ritual. By the method mentioned in the book, he needed to complete the sacrifices only on a no moon night.

After he managed to capture 1000 kids. He waited for the moonless night. Once the day had arrived he took the kids underground to complete the ritual but by that time the Headmaster and the rest of us got the information about what Charvik was about to do.

Charvik had by the time we reached had started the procession and murdered 300 kids. A fight ensued between us and Charvik and his followers. Charvik became more powerful than any of us. Even the headmaster was not able to tame him. By following Ipsit's methods, he had garnered more power as was mentioned in the book.

He was about to murder the rest of the kids when my headmaster executed his final mantra. He threw a mantra at Charvik and his followers. He froze them to stone. But it cost the headmaster his life.

But the spell could not hold Charvik longer. There was another method through which Charvik could immortalize himself. He could complete the sacrifices, piecemeal. That is, by offering sacrifices in the order 300+300+300+100. He would return every 300 years to complete the ritual each time sacrificing in that order. I tried to stop him from different generations and failed. This is the last time; I have a chance to rectify my sin of teaching him.

My Master had informed me to find the Golden Warrior. I tried so many times, and I failed each and every time.

This time this boy is coming to find the Golden Warrior. And I don't know what to do.'

Indranuj completed his explanation to Erish. Erish now understood why the Outsider had taken Asmi and the other kids as his captive. The Outsider intended to sacrifice Asmi and others to immortalize himself. Which meant if Erish did not find the Golden Warrior soon enough Asmi would die.

Erish had nearly spent one week in getting to Indranuj and he now only had a week to save Asmi.

Erish asked, 'So where do I find the Golden Warrior?'

Indranuj gave Erish a map and answered, 'Beyond this way', he pointed at the road leading into the woods, 'there is a river flowing downside. You need to follow the river. The river merges with the seven seas down there. You need to dive and go beneath the sea. There you will find The Golden Warrior!'

Erish exclaimed, 'I need to go to the depths of the sea?'

Indranuj asserted, 'Yes!'

Erish asked, 'But how can someone go someone so deep? I can't hold my breath for that long and I don't know how to swim.'

Indranuj answered, 'For that, you need to obtain the Water-Flower alongside the river bed you will go through' Indranuj pointed out the riverbed on the map, 'Here you have to collect the water-flower.'

Indranuj showed Erish a picture of how the Water-Flower looked. 'You need to keep them in handy. If you eat this flower you won't require air for a few hours and you don't need to swim. The water-flower contains magical properties. You will be able to swim as long as the power of water-flower rests in your belly. Then you can go below and get the sword.'

Erish nodded his head in agreement.

'Quick! Time is slipping by you need to keep going now! 'Indranuj said, 'Come with me.'

Indranuj led Erish to a flowing river. Erish saw that the river was flowing downside. A small boat was tied near the river. Indranuj undid the ropes of the boat and asked Erish to sit in it.

Indranuj said, 'Boy, my old age will not allow me to come with you. You need to get there fast. Take the map. It will show you the way.'

Erish sat in the boat. The river was carrying the boat along its way. Erish saw behind, Indranuj was standing there looking at him. Little by little, Indranuj had completely vanished. Erish sat there he held his bag near him. He was alone once again.

After Erish left. Indranuj had a task to complete. He had to pass the message further about Erish's arrival. Indranuj wrote a message: 'A boy is coming for the Golden Warrior' and put that piece of message on a plant near his window.

And muttered, 'By the powers vested in me, I command you to reach your destination.'

There was bright gold light and the plant absorbed the piece of paper. The message along with the paper vanished.

CHAPTER 11

Mahakethu along with a few of his followers were scanning the landscape for the boy with the twisted arm. Charvik had instructed him to bring the boy so that he can butcher him before his sister.

Mahakethu and others were on large birds scanning the horizon for the boy. Aghori had shown him last that he was on a boat along the river headed to the seven seas.

Mahakethu was now hovering above the riverbed looking for Erish.

Agathshatru was walking with the support of his long stick. He was striding fast to Yajin's chamber. Yajin was about to go to sleep.

Agathashatru had been pondering about it for long. He finally decided to act upon it.

Agathashatru knocked on Yajin's door. Yajin opened the door. He was surprised to see his Master this late.

'Master, what happened?' Yajin asked.

'Yajin, I need you to go to Giriraj and request him to give you the Golden Key. We will soon require the Golden Chamber to be opened. But the chamber is locked, Only the Golden Key can open the chamber.'

'I will leave right now, Master' Yajin asserted.

'My boy, I knew you will always obey me,' Agathashatru said.

And Yajin left with Onik that very moment to get to Giriraj.

Yajin muttered, 'By the powers vested in me, I command you to grow bigger.' A red light darted out of his hands towards Onik.

The mantra hit Onik and Onik was getting bigger and bigger.

After Onik became big enough for Yajin to sit upon it, Yajin stopped the mantra and sat upon Onik.

Onik took flight with one swift swoosh.

Agathashatru stood below as Yajin flew into the sky and disappeared.

Giriraj was deep in thought about what to do? Charvik was about to complete the final ritual in a week. He could not be defeated by anyone. Charvik was stronger and more powerful than before if he completes the ritual all will be over. He needed to stop Charvik and the only way to stop Charvik was by being summoning the Golden Warrior. The previous attempts of summoning the Golden Warrior have been in vain.

He struggled with the cost of what price people had to pay for summoning the Golden warrior. It was a price too heavy to pay that too with no guarantee of help from the Golden Warrior.

Giriraj clutched the locket he was wearing around his neck tighter. Struggling with what will be the right step.

He sighed wondering if Charvik could even be stopped.

And now this disciple had come from Agathashatru requesting for the Golden Key.

The disciple stated what Agathashatru had said, 'Giriraj, please give the Golden Key. That is our only hope to stop Charvik and protect the innocent kids.'

Giriraj was not to be persuaded so easily. He listened to Agathashatru's request before and witnessed what horrible things he had done.

He would not allow that to happen to any other innocent soul ever again. But the second option was even more horrible: Charvik would butcher all those kids and no one will be there to stop them.

Giriraj was in a dilemma.

Erish held the oar in his mouth and with the help of his one hand, he started steering the boat. He had opened the map, Indranuj gave him. Erish had been paying keen attention to his surroundings. He was afraid if crocodiles would come at him from underneath the water.

He also looked around if he could spot any water-flower around him. According to Indranuj's instructions, Erish chartered the river slowly without attracting the attention of any river monster. Indranuj had mentioned to him earlier that if he sees flowers blossoming around the riverside you have reached the riverbed.

It had been hours yet Erish was not able to reach the riverbed. Erish knew that with each passing hour his chances of saving Asmi were diminishing.

He looked once again at the Rakhi around his twisted arm. A reminder that a brother always protects his sister. Now all alone, he began to have doubts about whether he could protect his sister. All the things he had witnessed up until now were more powerful than he could ever be. And still some challenges remained before him. 'Only the Golden Warrior can save Asmi, I need to request the Golden Warrior to save Asmi, he is the only hope' He thought.

Memories came back to him. How he and his sister used to play in the school garden. How Asmi used to protect him from the school bullies who used to bully Erish and make fun of him over his twisted arm. How she cared for him when he was sick. How she applied balm on his legs when he got himself injured while playing.

All these thoughts occupied Erish's mind when the boat took speed. Erish was unaware of it, lost in his thoughts.

Erish came back to the present when he felt something hot approaching him from above. He looked above; it was a red fireball.

The fireball hit Erish's boat breaking the front side of the boat and burning it down completely.

Erish looked above to see what was happening. It was the Outsiders. They were hovering above them in big birds. One of them had hit him with a fireball.

First, they took his sister from him to kill her, and now they returned to kill him as well.

The boat could no longer hold itself on water. It was sinking as the water rushed from the broken side.

The boat was now gaining momentum. It was moving and sinking with equal speed. There were big bedrocks in the river. The river was tossing the sinking boat from one rock to the other.

Erish was trying to balance himself on the fast-moving sinking boat. Another ball of fire came from above missing him in inches.

Erish was slipping into the water as the boat was crumbling down evermore. Erish tried to move upwards in the direction of the boat. Water was eating into the whole boat.

The Outsiders were now diving below with their great birds.

One eagle hovered above the Erish and started to claw at him with its claws. Erish somehow dodged the claws of the eagle and balanced himself on the boat.

Several Outsiders circled the sinking the boat with the gigantic birds. Erish felt trapped amidst them. His boat was sinking and he was covered on all sides by the Outsiders.

The gigantic birds all started to clutch Erish in their claws missing him by millimetres. Erish was hit hard by a pointed claw of a bird. He lost his balance and fell into the river.

The river was pushing Erish in its current and pulling him to her depths. Erish went under the water, his legs and hand were fighting with all there might to beat the river current. He fanatically started beating his legs and arms in a desperate attempt to lift himself above the water.

He came above one moment and went below the next moment. Water rushed inside Erish's mouth as he opened his mouth for air. His twisted arm was not being helpful to him at all. The river crashed him against a bedrock. Erish tried to hold himself on the rock but it was too slippery.

The river swallowed Erish. Erish held his breath inside the river. Water rushed into his ears. Bringing all his energy together he pushed himself once again against the water to rise above it. He came up and took air into his starved lungs. It was only for a moment then he was down in the water gain. He looked in the direction where the river was taking him. There were big bedrocks on the riverway. He calculated and floated himself in such a way that he could hold onto a bedrock. He neared a bedrock and clutched himself on it.

The bedrock provided himself with enough support that he could take some breath but the Outsiders did not. They approached in their big birds and started clawing again. The fireballs were launched all around him.

Erish slipped into the water once again. The river was now flowing at its peak speed. Erish saw ahead and realized why the river was flowing so fast.

The river pulled Erish inside her. Erish had no energy left in him. His tiny body could not hold much longer. He needed air now. He opened his mouth for air and water gushed inside his mouth.

His lungs were filling with water instead of air. His mind stopped working and he went deeper and deeper into the river.

His vision was getting blurred. His senses were dulling. He looked at his twisted arm. The Rakhi his sister tied was still there. It reminded him that a brother always protects his sister. He looked forward and he saw something glittering. It was as if somebody was there. He could not make out who but someone was there. The image became more defined it looked like Avyay. Erish felt as if the image was speaking to him 'It doesn't matter how many hands you have got what matter is what you have got in the one you have got' The words Avyay told Erish also came back to him.

Suddenly he sprang back to life and started beating his hands and legs again. He started fighting the river with whatever was left inside him. He rolled his entire body to get above the water. He twisted and curled. And finally, he came above the water. This time he was not just beating his hands and legs, he was swimming. The near-death encounter had forced him to swim.

But his problems were not over. The Outsiders were still hovering above him. They targeted Erish with their giant birds like they were trying to catch a swimming fish.

One big eagle tried to dive directly at him. Erish dived beneath the water to escape its attack. There were several bedrocks there. The Eagle badly damaged itself against the rocks.

The Outsiders could not take a direct dive at Erish. So, they started hovering above and tried to clutch him the bird's claws. But each time they tried to do so Erish dived beneath.

And now Erish saw that the river was coming to an end, there was a waterfall ahead!

Erish had no other choice but to go with the flow.

And so, he did. He went with the flow and fell off with the water into the waterfall.

Mahakethu was hovering above the waterfall. The Waterfall was big. 'The boy cannot have a chance of surviving that fall' one of them muttered.

Yet Mahakethu still scanned the landscape if he could spot the boy. Neither the boy nor his body was to be seen.

Mahakethu had launched that fireball so that he could play with the boy for some time but the plan did not go as he had envisioned it. He thought the boy would fall in the river and then Mahakethu will pick him up and take him to Charvik.

After some wait, Mahakethu and others left the spot.

Mahakethu and others reached the palace. Charvik was seated in his chair. Charvik looked at his followers and asked, 'Where's the boy?'

'Charvik, we lost the boy. He fell off from the waterfall, there is no chance that he could survive that fall.' Mahakethu answered.

Charvik maintained a grim silence. 'It happens that boy failed to protect himself how could he protect his sister.'

Charvik dismissed the boy with the twisted arm from his thoughts.

The predator was chasing the stag. The Stag was running at its top speed to avoid being the lunch of the predator.

The stag cleverly ran into the bushes and was outrunning the predator. The predator was unable to run any longer, exhausted by the chase went back empty-handed.

The stag took a breather when the lion was no longer at its back. It was thirsting for water. He could hear the distant sound of a voice nearby.

It followed the voice of the water and reached the stream of water. Its instincts told it to look around for any dangers. After careful examination it went near the water, it glanced sideways to make sure nothing was there in the water.

After making sure it was safe, it lowered its neck and started to quelch its thirst. It opened its eyes while drinking and saw a pair of eyes getting closer. The creature within the water suddenly leaped up at the stag.

The stag ran away from the creature in the water.

After establishing a safe distance, the stag saw the creature inside the flowing water. This creature was unlike anything the stag had seen in its life.

A hand had suddenly leaped from the water and was pushing itself across the river bed. It was Erish.

CHAPTER 12

Erish had managed to survive the waterfall. He came out of the river and took shelter in the nearby big banyan tree.

He was all wet. He removed his map from his bag both the bag and the map were wet. The map became so thin that it was torn from the middle.

With great care, Erish handled the map and took a look at it.

As Indranuj had instructed him earlier. He had successfully crossed the waterfall. He looked around him. There were flowers: Golden Flowers.

He remembered Indranuj saying, 'It is easy to recognize the Water-flower: It is the only flower that is of Golden Colour. If you can see golden coloured flowers that means you have reached the riverbed. Collect as many water-flowers as you can and get moving along the river. The river will merge with the seven seas. And then you need to go down.'

Erish had successfully dodged the Outsiders and reached the river-bed. Now what was left was to collect the water-flower and go beneath the seven seas.

He looked at the map. The seven seas were not far away from the river bed. He needed to pace up.

Without wasting much time, he started collecting the water-flowers and started packing it in his bag. The water-flower was glittering in the sunlight. It was crisp and soft. Erish never saw any flower like this. There was much in this world, he had never seen before.

After packing his bag with the Water-flowers, he started making his boat. He needed some sort of boat to travel the river and reach the seven seas.

The wicked Outsiders had destroyed his boat and tried to kill him above the waterfall. He would approach the Golden Warrior and save his sister and also take his revenge on the Outsiders for trying to kill him.

Erish collected some fallen branches from the trees and some woods nearby. He needed some wire to tie the wood together. He searched for something akin to the wire. He found creepers hanging from the trees. He collected those creepers and used it to tie his wood together.

He had learned in his school how to prepare your little boat when you were lost near any river.

With great effort and with the help of only one hand he made his tiny boat.

He slipped the handmade boat into the water and it was floating well on it. He took another wood to use it as an oar.

Then he took his bag and seated on his boat he started oaring towards the seven seas.

Bakula stood near the Golden Sword. The Sword so many tried to pick so many failed. A few succeeded but failed later. And now he just kept looking at the sword.

Earlier this morning. While he was sipping some tea. The plant near him brought a message. Bakula had not received any message from long. Bakula's father was guarding the sword and his grandfather earlier. Bakula inherited the responsibility of guarding the Golden Sword against his father.

Bakula's father had told him while he was still alive that someone in his family lineage was a student of a certain Agathashatru. That lineage was given the responsibility of guarding the golden sword. The sword was to be used only to kill the evil. And the sword will not allow anyone to pick it except the one whose will is strong.

The sword would test the will of the person horrifically.

Bakula opened the piece of the message he obtained earlier. It was scribbled on it: Some boy was coming for the Golden Warrior!

The message surprised Bakula at first. 'Some boy?!' he thought.

Then later when he saw Erish through his bowl of seawater fighting the stream of the river, dodging the outsiders, and surviving the fall from the waterfall, collecting the water-flower, building a boat all by himself despite a twisted arm and sailing right towards the seven seas to get the Golden Warrior, he thought the boy was strong-willed.

But his opinion did not matter. The Golden Sword would test the boy's will and at that time the boy should be strong-willed.

Bakula wondered if the boy could withstand the pain and the shock.

His mind was full of thoughts he came to the mouth of his cave and looked outside. It was filled with seawater. His cave was in the depths of the seven seas. Through tantric mantra's he had stopped the seawater from entering his cave.

He looked at the seawater and was lost in thoughts.

Agathashatru waited outside his dark palace. He was waiting for Yajin to return. Then far away in the clouds, he saw Ovin spreading his wings coming back along with Yajin. Yajin was seated on the Owl's back.

Ovin recognized Agathashatru and hooted.

Yajin made Ovin land near Agathashatru.

Agathashatru asked earnestly, 'Yajin?! Did Giriraj gave the Golden Key?'

Yajin could see the desperate hope in Agathashatru's face. He felt helpless in saying it, 'Giriraj refused to give the Golden Key.'

Agathashatru was saddened at the news. He knew however that Giriraj was not someone who would change his mind once he made it.

'Who could blame him after all that I made him witness?' Agathashatru thought.

'Master, he told me something to tell you,' Yajin said to Agathashatru.

Agathashtru asked, 'What is it?'

'He told me he would test the one who came for the Golden Key himself,' Yajin answered.

'So be it,' Aghathashatru exclaimed.

Erish crossed the river and darted the ship into the seven seas.

Erish remembered Indranuj saying to him the last time they were together. 'When you enter the seven seas, you wouldn't have time to get to the middle of the seven seas. You need to use Tantrism then.

Indranuj scribbled a mantra on a piece of paper and gave it to Erish.

Erish removed the piece of paper from his pocket and uttered the spell:

'By the powers vested in me, I command the sea's to take me to the one whose name is Bakula!'

Erish waited for a couple of minutes in silence. Nothing happened.

Then slowly but steadily he felt the sea was pulling his boat. He saw the waves moving in the opposite direction.

He saw that the sea was now forming a vortex and gaining momentum. Erish held onto his boat tighter. The sea waves now came crashing into him. His boat was being carried away by sea. He saw ahead of him the sea pulling him faster and faster.

He and his boat were cutting through the wind. Salty water went into Erish's mouth.

The momentum reached its deadly peak the boat was now being pulled at a speed Erish had never witnessed before.

He was surrounded by humongous waves all around him. the water was flashing from one side to the other. The wind and the waves made an exhilarating combination.

Erish could not make out what was happening before him. Erish strained his eyes to look at what was happening ahead of him.

Then he saw that the sea was devouring him. Ahead of him, the water formed a rotating tunnel and it was sucking everything around it.

He immediately pulled the Water-flowers from his backpack and swallowed as many as he could. The taste of the water-flower was very salty. He felt a strange sensation in his body. He felt lite. It was as if his lungs were full of oxygen and he didn't need anymore.

In a blink of an eye, the sea sucked Erish. Erish once again was submerged under the seawater and was tossed beneath and beneath.

He held his breath and closed his eyes and let the sea did whatever it was doing.

Bakula watched from the cave as the sea was bringing the boy with the twisted arm to him. The sea was circling itself and the boy was circling in the seawater. The sea dropped the boy at the cave.

Bakula went near the boy. The boy was all wet soaked in salty seawater.

Erish looked up at the figure looming above him and asked, ' Are you the Golden Warrior?'

Bakula answered, 'No, I am not the Golden Warrior!'

All the hopes of Erish disappeared at that statement.

Here he was, searching desperately for the Golden Warrior so that he could protect his sister, crossing obstacles, overcoming his handicapped, and still, his quest for the Golden Warrior did not seem to end.

Erish knew that he had very little time now that the fortnight was nearing him. He had to discover the Golden Warrior quickly.

Bakula saw the disappointment on the boy's face.

Bakula consoled Erish, 'Kid! You don't have much time. Don't be disappointed. You are closer to the Golden Warrior now than ever before. But to summon the Golden Warrior you need the Golden sword.'

Bakula waited to see if Erish was able to grasp the meaning behind his words.

Erish absorbed the meaning behind his words.

When Bakula realized that the boy had grasped his words he asked, 'Kid! Come with me!'

Erish entered the Cave which was Bakula's home. Erish turned back and saw that seawater did not enter the cave. He was nonplussed by that scene.

Erish went along with the figure who was leading him deeper and deeper into the cave. This old man was similar to the old man he has been meeting since he set upon his quest for the Golden Warrior.

Erish had a creepy feeling inside the walls of the cave. They were all lonely and ghostlike. Erish wondered if this old man lived here all alone.

They reached an intersection of different paths within the cave, and Bakula proceeded to go ahead in one of the paths.

Erish followed suit.

The path was getting narrower and narrower and darker and darker as they moved ever so close deeper and deeper.

Erish couldn't make out for how long he has been walking along with this old man before him. He couldn't see anything clearly in the dark. The only thing he could see is the silhouette of the man that was moving in front of him.

Finally, Bakula stopped at one point.

Erish also stopped right beside him. Unable to know what was going on.

'By the powers vested in me, I command thyself to light up!' Bakula roared.

A sudden gleam of light spread inside that dark spot. The light was so bright that Erish had to close his eyes to stop excessive light from entering his eyes. It was flashing and flashing lights like thunder balls.

After a few moments, Light was evenly distributed in that spot and Erish opened his eyes slowly.

Erish saw that he was in some sort of a big circular chamber. And in the middle of that circular chamber was a Golden Sword thrusted into the ground. And a few feet away from the sword were piles of dead decomposing human bodies, some so old that their skeletons were visible too.

Erish was frightened by the piled of dead bodies. No wonder he had been feeling creepy about this place and it felt like ghostlike.

Bakula went near the Golden Sword and kneeled before it. He was looking at it intently.

'Erish!' Bakula said.

This was the first time Bakula had used Erish's name.

'Come to her,' Bakula ordered.

Erish obeyed. Circumspecting the dead bodies, he carefully went near Bakula.

Bakula was still keenly looking at the sword.

Bakula continued, 'This is the Golden sword. The Sword of the Golden Warrior!'

Erish looked at the sword. There was something inexplicably attractive about that sword. Erish could sense that the sword contained some powers within it.

Bakula narrated, his eyes still on the sword, 'In your quest for the Golden Warrior, you will need this sword. The sword contains unimaginable powers. It was built by the debris of the dead bodies of the tantrics. To summon the Golden Warrior, you will need to present him with the Golden Sword. But the sword does not give itself up to anyone. Only the strong-willed can pull the sword from the ground. But the sword will not allow anyone to pull itself up that easily. There will be a test to see how strong your will is and how deep your need is.'

Bakula maintained a few moments of silence and continued, 'So many have tried to pull this sword and only a few succeeded in pulling the sword. The debris of dead bodies is of warriors who came before you to pull the sword but failed.'

Bakula turned his head towards Erish. Erish looked at Bakula.

Bakula said, 'I hope you will not end up like them. As you can see it is a very nasty job to pile up bodies in one part of this chamber.'

Erish didn't know how to respond to that remark.

'So, are you ready to pull the sword?!' Bakula asked Erish.

'I ought to be, my sister doesn't have much time. That Outsider, Charvik, will murder her in two days if I don't get the Golden Warrior soon.' Erish spoke.

'all right kid. Then pull the sword with all that you have got.'

'What will happen to me when I pull the sword?'

'The Sword will test you if you worthy or not,' Bakula answered.

Erish neared the Golden Sword. He readied himself for it. He took a deep breath, held his hand against the grip of the sword, and started pulling it out.

'Ahhhhh!' Erish loosened his grip on the sword.

No sooner had Erish pulled the sword from the ground a massive golden shock wave passed through his body.

His arm felt numb for some seconds. The shock wave was utterly unexpected. 'The sword must be testing me' Erish thought.

'You don't have time kid, quickly try again,' Bakula ordered.

Mustering up some courage, Erish prepared himself once again and held the grip on the sword and pulled it from the ground.

As expected, another massive shock wave passed through him, but this time he wasn't going to lose his grip so soon. He lifted the sword a little higher. The sword was heavy enough for him with the added benefit of this shock wave passing through his body.

'Ahh!' Erish screamed but held his grip and pulled even higher.

Another massive wave of shock passed through his body. He lost his grip a little bit. Finally, the shock wave overpowered his convictions and he lost his grip on the sword.

His whole body was now feeling numb and dizzy. He lost his balance and sat silently on the ground. His whole body shaking with the shock he had experienced.

Slowly, he opened his fist off his arm with which he held the sword and now he saw that there was a burn mark on his palm. His skin burnt with the shock wave.

His mind was trying hard to retain his sense. He wanted to try once again but his body was not allowing him to try.

Bakula gushingly held Erish's hand and said, 'Boy, you have to try. The sword is testing you. It is testing your will, how strong your will is, how strongly you want the sword. Muster all your will and pull the sword.'

The words of Bakula was dizzying in Erish's mind.

Bakula held Erish's hand was shaking him.

'Erish! Erish!' Bakula said. Erish's senses were dulling.

'Wake up! You need…golden warrior. For your sister…save her. You can…'

Erish was far from able to comprehend what was Bakula saying.

Bakula saw that Erish was losing his consciousness. He tried whatever he could to wake him up. He was shaking Erish by his twisted arm.

'Erish! Wake up!'

Erish came to his senses for a brief moment. His body was weakened by the massive shock waves. He looked at the figure before him who was desperately trying to wake him up. He also saw his twisted arm. There was a mark on his twisted arm. The mark where the rakhi had been. The rakhi his sister tied him a couple of days ago.

Memories came back to him.

Avyay was angry at Erish. He strode towards Erish and asked in an angry tone, 'Why did you not pick up the Sword?'

Erish tried to answer, 'I was scared. The Sword was too heavy for me. I only have one hand.' Erish gestured to his twisted right hand.

Avyay pulled Erish's left hand and spoke his voice was still angry, 'It doesn't matter how many hands you have got; what matters is what you have got in the one you have got.' He said pressing Erish's hand. 'These stupid sea dragons are nothing,' Avyay said kicking a dead sea dragon beside him, 'in front of what you will be facing coming ahead. And that time if you cry 'I have got only hand' YOU WILL DIE! If you fail to act at the decisive time then Your Sister Will Die! If you want to convince the Golden Warrior to come to your sister rescue then having only one hand will be the least of your troubles.'

Avyay levelled himself at Erish's height and looked him straight in the eye. The rays of the sun fell upon him and gave him a golden aura. Avyay just kept looking at Erish. The wind was blowing near them. The wind ruffled Avyay's long hair. Then Avyay said with strictness, 'Erish! I going to tell you something which I want you to remember.'

Erish nodded his head in agreement.

Avyay continued, 'What I am going to tell you is very important for you, for your quest for the Golden Warrior, and in protecting your Sister's life.'

Erish muttered in a low voice, ' All right.'

Then Avyay muttered two words to Erish. Words Erish would never forget for the rest of his life.

CHAPTER 13

Erish jolted back to life. His body recuperated from the shock. Bakula saw the boy before him. He looked into his eyes and saw 'determination'.

Erish stood up though his body was still weak. He looked at his twisted arm at the mark that was still there of the rakhi that which his sister tied to him.

He raised his other arm and recalled the words of Avyay, 'It doesn't matter how many hands you have got; what matters is what you have got in the one you have got.'

He looked at the Golden Sword before him and rushed towards it.

Taking a deep breath and using all his might he held the golden sword and pulled it with all his might.

New shock waves emerged from the golden sword. One after another but Erish held his ground. Each time a new shock wave attacked Erish, He would pull the sword even higher.

'Aaaaahhh!' Erish screamed when the shock wave passed through him but did not lose his grip.

The sword was being pulled ever higher from the ground.

Bakula saw the spectre before him. The boy was winning the test. The sword was testing the will of the boy and the boy was proving how strong his will was.

There was one final test pending, and Bakula knew that Erish was nearing that test.

Just when Erish was about to pull the sword completely out from the ground. The final and the most lethal shock wave passed through him.

'Arghhh!' Erish roared.

This was the most gigantic shock Erish would receive. The Final Shock Wave.

The shock was paralyzing his tiny body yet he soldiered on.

Erish closed his eyes and mustered his full will to the task.

Agathashatru opened his eyes. His past was haunting him. He was seated on the stairs outside the tantric mansion. His mind was occupied by a series of thoughts.

He remembered in vivid detail the choices he made in life. The choices he was not supposed to make. The choices that have culminated to bring him nightmares for the rest of his life.

He could still hear her voice. That lovely voice that made him fall in love with her. He recalled how she looked and how they looked together.

He remembered how much shame he would have brought to his Master and so he hid his shame. Only to realize at the end that his shame would return to get even.

The humiliation he caused. The ostracize he caused. All because of his choice.

The words his master told him once came to his mind now, 'If at all you have made a choice that you know is the wrong one. Admit it and bear its consequences. Lest you will not be able to either bear the consequences or admit it.'

Fool he was! Agathashatru reprimanded himself. 'I should have admitted my choice back then and bore the consequences and now as my Master told I am neither able to bear the consequence nor admit it.'

He stood up with great effort. His thoughts were consuming too much of his energy. He walked alone for some time.

Yajin saw his master Agathashatru taking a walk. Yajin realized that his Master needed solitude now more than ever.

Yajin was able to assemble the pieces of the puzzle to understand what was happening around him. He needed a few more pieces, a few more information to completely see the picture for what it was.

Giriraj's disciple fetched some water for his Master.

'Master', he asked, 'what is happening here? First, that man arrived called Charvik and now this strange exchange of messages. And the visit by that lad Yajin who wanted the key you are wearing across your neck. And your refusal to give it.'

Giriraj answered, 'To understand what is happening now. You need to go back to more than 300 years ago.'

Saying so, Giriraj swiped his hand from left to right in the air and an image appeared before him in mid-air.

The disciple came closer and he could see the events happening 300 years ago.

'Fire was consuming him while the man screamed in unbearable pain. Stop it Please Stop it the man bemoaned but none of the group of the tantrics who were performing the ritual stopped. For them, the cries of pain and mercy were not audible while they were obsessed with their desires.

The man's body was twisting and curling to protect himself from the devouring fire. But all his attempts were in vain. The fire would find one way or the other to enter inside him.

'Noooooo!' The man roared in pain. But the group of tantrics who surrounded the man were having none of his pleas.

The fire entered the man's mouth and started burning him from the inside. The man-made terrible noises when his innards were being burnt by the fire.

The strange verses the tantrics were reciting were growing louder and louder and so was the power of the fire that was consuming the man alive.

The man was eclipsed completely in the ball of fire. He thrashed his legs and arms wildly to fight the ongoing slaughter by fire but without results.

The tantrics were all wearing black hoods and robes that covered them fully. There were several of the tantrics united by a single goal. To burn that man to ashes, it seemed.

It took several painful moments for the ritual to complete while the man was dropped down by the fire.

The man whatever the tantrics had planned to do with him had died.'

The disciple observed closely at all the tantrics who were performing this deadly ritual and found the one he was hoping not to find: Giriraj.

Just then Giriraj closed the window that was playing that past event.

The Disciple was speechless. 'Master?! Is it that? And what were you doing there? Did you do it? Is that man murdered by you all…?'

Giriraj was disgusted by himself.

'Agathashatru persuaded me to do it. It was one life versus the life of 300 innocent kids. I thought he knew what was happening. Only later did I and others whom he had persuaded had realized that the ritual was costly and with no guarantees of yielding results.' Giriraj spoke.

'After that incident, I vowed along with a few others.' Continued Giriraj, 'never to trust Agathashatru. And to find an alternate solution to the evil intentions of Charvik.'

'You mean to say, you tried stopping Charvik earlier as well?'

'Yes! But we failed that time. And thought that we would succeed in taming Charvik this time but even after 300 years of patience and hard work we have not found any solution.'

'And now?'

'And now, Agathashatru wants to redo the process once again to stop Charvik,' Giriraj answered.

'Arghh!' Erish used all his might. The shock wave passed through him yet he clutched himself to the sword with his only arm and pulled it ever higher.

Flashes of golden light fell over Bakula. The entire circular room was vibrating with the shock waves and golden lighting.

The floor beneath him was shaking. He could feel the strength of the Golden Sword.

And in one swift motion, Erish pulled the Golden Sword from the ground.

Erish held the Golden Sword in his hand. He could feel how mighty the sword was. 'If the Sword is so powerful then I wonder how powerful the one who holds it, The Golden Warrior! must be.' Erish thought.

Erish felt renewed energy flowing in his veins. He felt as if all the energy he had expended had returned to him as tenfold.

He looked at Bakula. Bakula looked back at him and smiled.

'You have succeeded in the test,' Bakula affirmed. 'And now you have to go to the one whose name is the Golden Warrior!'

Saying so he recited another verse in the Golden Warrior Puzzle:

' The one who refuses to give up,

Even when he is fallen,

The one who stands up,

Even when he is beaten,

He can be found by following the moon,

He's the one named 'The Golden Warrior!'

Bakula completed his verse.

'What is the meaning of it? Where do I go now? Where to find the Golden Warrior?' Erish asked in his tiny voice.

'You need to follow the moon. It is already night. Come my way, I will show you.' Bakula said.

Bakula then ventured back to the way from where they came. Erish followed Bakula, the Golden Sword still in his hand.

They reached the earlier intersection where two paths diverged. Bakula stopped there.

Erish came behind Bakula and saw the other way.

Bakula kept looking the other way and said, 'Go kid. You need to save your sister. Go through this tunnel. It will lead outside and then there will be a monastery. There you will find the Golden Warrior!'

Erish looked into the tunnel ahead, it was all dark.

Bakula gave Erish a scabbard to keep his Golden Sword and bade him goodbye.

Erish nodded and ventured into the dark tunnel, in search of the one, whose name is The Golden Warrior!

After Erish left, Bakula felt a strangeness in his abode. As if he was all alone once again. But he had a task to do.

He immediately scribbled a few words on a piece of paper. He was wearing a locket that had a human skull like structure around his neck. He held the piece of paper in front of the locket and muttered, 'By the powers vested in me, I command you to deliver the message.'

There was a bright light emerged from the skull. And the skull ate the piece of paper.

After that, the light disappeared and everything went black.

Giriraj was staring down at his reflection in the little pond. He could see the Golden Key hanging from his neck. He looked closely at the inscription on it. It was worded in Sanskrit. He knew that this was the key to defeat Charvik.

He reminded himself of the previous times when the key was used and the disastrous consequence that followed.

A bright light emerged from the water below. Giriraj closed his eyes because of excess light. And then a small piece of paper emerged from the water.

'A message'. Giriraj thought.

He picked the piece of paper and read it:

'Somebody is coming for the Golden Key.'

 A crowd of bats flew towards Erish. Erish held up his hand to cover his head. The tunnel was getting darker and darker as he moved forward to the other side of the tunnel. He was barely able to see anything.

At one point, he wished if he had a torch of some sort to navigate this dark tunnel. As soon as he wished the Golden Sword he was holding in his scabbard started glowing brighter.

Erish took the sword out and the brightness from the sword lightened the whole tunnel.

'The Sword it heard my wish.' Erish thought.

With the tunnel lighted, Erish strode fast to get to the other side. He had little time left. He needed to go fast and find the Golden Warrior.

After some time, he could see light emerging at the far end of the tunnel. He realized he was nearing the end of the tunnel.

Putting his sword back in his scabbard, he dashed towards the opening of the tunnel.

Trees, Flowers, and Grass decorated the landscape. He reached the woods as Bakula had mentioned earlier.

He looked up and above towards the monastery that was there on the small hill.

He started running there to save his sister to get help from the one whose name is the Golden Warrior.

Charvik tasted the food made by his mother. She was loving and kind in a cruel and heartless world. She used to nurse him when he was sick, took care of him when everyone abused and hated him.

She worked hard for him while his father abandoned them.

He remembered how it felt growing up as a fatherless child. How it felt when others had taunted him as a bastard.

He vowed one day he would take revenge on all of them. And he did it.

It felt oddly satisfying to see the terror on the faces of all those men who at one time had thrashed him away. Only to find he would grow stronger and more powerful than anyone of them could have imagined.

He took his revenge slowly torturing them seeing them cry in pain he felt happy.

He still remembered the episode with his mother that changed his life forever. She had never revealed to him who was his father. Yet Charvik persisted in asking about the whereabouts of his father.

He remembered asking his mother as a child, 'When will father come home?!'

He always used to get the same answer from his mother, 'Father is away on work. He will come soon.'

And Charvik waited and waited for his father to return but he never showed up.

Then one fine day, his mother fell ill from an incurable disease when he was still 10 years old. He was not able to save his mother back then. Back then he was weak, devoid of any tantric powers to save his mother.

On realizing that her death was imminent she spoke to her only son about something very important. On her final day, she revealed the secret she had kept to herself till then to Charvik.

And showed Charvik a way to live in this world. Little did she knew then that without her guidance what path Charvik was about to take.

Erish reached the monastery running faster. An old man was seated near the entrance gate guarding it.

The Old man saw Erish coming towards him. He stood up and strode towards Erish.

Erish reached the old man and before he could say anything the old man asked him, 'Did you come for the Golden Warrior?!'

Giriraj had informed the old man earlier that somebody was coming for the Golden Warrior. The Old Man had expected some grown-up man and not a handicapped child.

'Yes! I have to save my sister.' Erish spoke trying to catch some breath due to his running, ' I don't have much time. Can you please take me to the Golden Warrior!'

The old man was confused about whether Erish was the one Giriraj was talking about. Giriraj has mentioned that he got a message saying, 'Somebody was coming for the Golden Warrior.'

But the one before him was not somebody but a small kid with a disabled hand hanging from his side.

The Old man asked, 'Did you pulled the Golden Sword?'

Erish nodded his head.

'Show me the Golden Sword.' The Old man ordered.

Erish took the Golden Sword from his scabbard and showed it to the Old Man.

The Old man looked closely at the inscriptions on the sword. It's carving and it's built. He took it in his hands and at once a massive shock wave pass through him and he dropped the sword down.

He dropped to his knees in pain. He saw his hand with which he had gripped the sword. There was a burnt mark at that place.

'But of course, The Golden Sword will not allow anyone else to hold it other than the one who pulled it.' The old man thought.

'Come with me.' Saying so the old man unlocked the entrance gate and Erish went inside the monastery.

Giriraj was waiting eagerly inside his chamber. He was still thinking of the dilemma. Should he let it happen or should he stop it?

 The old man and Erish reached Giriraj's chamber. The old man asked Erish to wait outside the chamber.

Giriraj observed his chamber door opened and the old man he had assigned to guard the gates had returned.

Giriraj looked at the old man for the news.

The old man answered, 'As you had mentioned earlier he has come for the Golden Warrior! He is waiting outside.'

Giriraj stood up and drew his strong long shiny Sword which was hanging on the wall.

'I will test him myself' Giriraj thought. 'Is he that strong?! That mighty! That he could have pulled off the Golden Sword.' He imagined how muscular and sturdy his hands would be! How manly would he look?!

Thinking these thoughts, he stepped outside his chamber to look at the mighty man who was looking for the Golden Warrior!

Giriraj looked ahead to have a look at the man. But no one was to be found there.

The Old man said to Giriraj, 'Giriraj, you have to look down.'

Giriraj looked down and he saw Erish watching at him.

CHAPTER 14

'Whoa!' Erish thought looking at the man's built. He was so muscular and mighty. Much muscular than Avyay.' Certainly, he must be the Golden Warrior' Erish thought.

'Can you please save my sister Asmi? That Outsider…Charvik he took her with him. Only you can save her? I have come a long way for you. Please Please help me.' Erish spoke non-stop.

Giriraj dropped his jaw looking at Erish. He looked back at the old man and asked, 'Is he the one searching for the Golden Warrior?'

The Old man answered, 'Apparently Yes. He is also carrying the Golden Sword with him. I tested it. The Golden Sword is allowing the boy to hold it.'

Giriraj stammered looking at the boy, 'But...But he is a kid!'

Giriraj bent on his knees and levelled himself with Erish. Placing a gentle hand upon Erish he asked, 'What's your name kid?'

'Erish' Erish answered.

'So, tell me Erish. Why do you need the Golden Warrior!'

Erish repeated once again, 'Can you please save my sister Asmi? That Outsider…Charvik he took her with him. Only you can save her? I have come a long way for you. Please Please help me.'

'Kid I am not the Golden Warrior!' Giriraj replied.

All the hopes of Erish were dashed. Giriraj could see the look of disappointment on Erish's face.

'But Bakula told me that after I pull off the Golden Sword, I will get to meet the Golden Warrior.' Erish iterated.

'Did he?' Giriraj wondered, 'Well you can meet the Golden Warrior kid.'

'Where can I meet him?' Erish asked.

'In the Golden Chamber.'

'The Golden Chamber? Where is the Golden Chamber?'

'I will tell you where is the Golden Chamber but before that, you need to have something?'

'What is that?'

'The Golden Key!' Giriraj spoke, 'The Golden Warrior is inside the Golden Chamber. And to summon him you need to open the doors of the Golden Chamber and you can only do so if you have the Golden Key!'

Erish absorbed whatever Giriraj was telling him. And his eyes felt upon the locket that Giriraj was wearing. He saw the Golden Key hanging around Giriraj's neck.

Pointing towards it, Erish asked, 'Is that the Golden Key?'

Giriraj looked at the key hanging from his neck shining brightly. He answered, 'Yes!'

'Please give me the Golden Key and tell me where is the Golden Chamber. I don't have much time. I need the Golden Warrior to save my sister.' Erish spoke.

Erish saw the change in Giriraj's face. From being tender and considerate, it became hard and stubborn.

'It's not that easy kid. For me to give you the Golden Key. You need to prove that you have what it takes to be worthy of it. You have pulled the Golden Sword successfully but the test you will be facing ahead would much more brutal and painful than what you have encountered till now. You need to do whatever it takes to save your sister. You don't have the luxury to step back. Will you do whatever it takes to save your sister?'

Erish tried to understand what Giriraj was trying to say and answered, 'I will.'

'Good! If you want the Golden Key and the address to the Golden Chamber then you have to duel me and defeat me.' Giriraj challenged.

Erish accepted the challenge.

Giriraj stood tall with a sword drawn in his hand in the ground of the monastery. Erish was on the opposite side with his Golden Sword.

The disciples and staff of the monastery surround Giriraj and Erish to see the duel.

Erish held the Golden Sword in his only hand and charged to attack at Giriraj.

Giriraj blocked the attack and punched Erish with the pommel of the sword.

Erish received a bloody cheek. It was painful yet he attacked Giriraj for a second time.

Again, this time, Giriraj blocked the attack and broke Erish's nose.

Erish cried in pain. Blood was dripping from his nose.

Giriraj came closer to Erish while Erish was struggling with the pain in his and landed another punch on his head.

Erish fell in pain.

Giriraj's disciple could see that Giriraj does not want to beat the kid but he was doing it for some reason.

Giriraj was about to land another blow when Erish saw it and ran away from the blow.

The pain was still bothering Erish. Blood still dripping from his cheek and his nose.

Giriraj was a master when it came to sword fighting, he had no chance of beating him yet he had no choice but to try if he had to save Asmi.

So, gathering himself up once again he launched an attack on Giriraj screaming.

Giriraj diverted the attack and this time landed a blow on Erish's eye.

Erish's eye burst in pain and he fell to the ground crying and roaring in pain. He lost the grip on his sword and was tumbling on the ground out of pain.

The disciples were aghast they had never seen Giriraj beat someone so brutally. And here he was almost killing the kid.

'Is this all? You cannot save your sister kid. Go back home.' Giriraj said to Erish.

Erish heard it. Mustering himself up he got on his feet. His head was covered in blood. 'I will fight.' He declared.

Giriraj took a deep breath and ran towards Erish and smashed his legs. Erish lost his balance and fell.

'It's over kid,' Giriraj said.

'Not yet,' Erish said and tried getting to his feet once again.

His vision was blurring now. He lost his one eye. He could only see so much from his one eye. Taking balance from his one hand he stood back on his feet.

Giriraj was staring back at him.

Erish saw the big hand of Giriraj bringing the pommel of the sword on his head.

'Bang!' Erish felt his skull breaking up. And he fell to the ground once again.

It was clear to Erish now. He could not defeat Giriraj. He has only one option and that was to beg Giriraj to give him the Golden Key.

'Please give me the Golden Key. I have to save my sister Asmi.'

Giriraj heard the plea but conflicting emotions were depicted on his face. And then he made his decision.

Erish could read the answer on Giriraj's face. It was 'No'.

With no other option left Erish tried to get back on his feet.

But Giriraj delivered another blow and Erish fell back on the ground.

The disciples watched with astonishment as Erish tried to get back again on his feet with whatever little was left in him even as Giriraj beat him again and again to the ground.

Erish fell to the ground once again. And once again he tried to the getup. And once again Giriraj shoved him back to the ground.

No matter how many times Giriraj beat the boy struggled to get back again on his feet.

Out of frustration, Giriraj beat the kid black and blue screaming, 'Stay Down.'

But Erish refused to stay down. He got up every goddamn time.

Giriraj inflicted bruising cuts with his sword on Erish's leg so that he stops getting up.

Erish fell. Not moving anymore.

'It's over Kid,' Giriraj answered.

 Observing that Erish was not moving anymore. Giriraj started heading back to his chambers.

Just then, He felt his disciples were astonished. Even without looking back, he knew Erish had gotten back on his feet.

He turned back to see Erish painfully moving towards him.

Giriraj strode closer to Erish and kicked him down.

Erish was tossed to the ground. Erish lay there without moving.

Giriraj sensing that the boy wouldn't get up again turned around and began to leave.

But he stopped midway. He saw in front of him. The sun had cast a long shadow of Erish across the wall.

He could see the shadow of Erish trying to get back on his feet.

He waited there motionless. Then he felt Erish hand grasp his hand.

He turned around to see the little boy dripped in blood clutching his finger and requesting, 'Please give me the Golden Key!'

Giriraj saw the butchered face. The only hand of Erish and the twisted arm. His bloody face, his one eyeball busted. His cheek bruised and his head fractured with the blows.

Giriraj was motionless just watching Erish. Then without a thought, he clutched the locket hanging from his neck and broke it away, and handed it to Erish.

Erish took the Golden Key and looked at it. He was exhausted of all energy. Panting to breathe. While all the other disciples saw the persistence of the little boy.

Giriraj took a deep breath and recited the final verse:

' The one who brings hope,

When hope is chopped,

The one who brings life,

When life is choked.

He can be found by crossing death,

He is the one named the Golden Warrior!'

Erish did not understand the verse. So, he looked up at Giriraj.

Giriraj said, 'We don't have much time. Charvik would initiate and complete the ritual by tonight. If we don't get there fast we will lose.'

'Order the flying beast to come over,' Giriraj ordered.

Some of his disciples went out to get the flying beast while the other disciples were nursing Erish's wounds.

A sudden gust of wind came from above.

Erish saw upwards and saw a massive black bird land on the ground. The bird was similar to those the Outsiders had arrived in.

 The disciples finished nursing Erish. Giriraj picked the little boy and placed him upon the bird.

'The flying beast would take you fast to the Golden Chamber! You don't have much time kid. Go save your sister.' Giriraj bade farewell to Erish...

Erish nodded his head and clinging hard to the flying beast he took off with the Golden Sword and the Golden Key for the one whose name is the Golden Warrior!

After Erish took his flight, one disciple asked Giriraj, 'Why do you beat the kid so badly?'

'Because I wanted to know something,' Giriraj replied.

'And what is that?'

'I wanted to see if the boy was ready to die for his sister. The boy proved he was! So, I gave him the Golden Key.'

The disciple asked a little shaken 'Will the boy die?'

Giriraj answered grimly, 'There is a cost to be paid to summon the Golden Warrior! That price is very costly. Sooner or later, in one way or another, the boy will die.'

CHAPTER 15

Erish was above the clouds. The flying beast was flying at the fury's pace. He clutched himself tightly against it. He had only a couple of hours left to save Asmi from Charvik. He had to get to the Golden Warrior fast. The wind was ruffling his hair in the flight. The beast was taking him above and above hills and mountains. Crossing lakes and rivers. All the while he was unaware that someone was watching him from somewhere.

Agathashatru watched in his bowl of water as Erish was nearing his tantric mansion for the Golden Warrior. He had already witnessed how much the boy persevered against the blows of Giriraj. And now Agathahsatru had to finally commit his sin once more, one more murder to stop Charvik. And so would he.

Yajin along with others were besides Agathashatru. He was worried if the process failed even this time. He asked Agathashatru not to do it. But the boy Erish, he was ready to do whatever it took to save his sister. 'If the boy was ready to die then so be it,' Agathahstru said.

Yajin learned recently the price of summoning the Golden Warrior is death. Only by dying can the Golden Warrior be summoned.

'You know Yajin when I was young I committed a terrible sin,' Agathashatru told Yajin. 'I fell in love with a beautiful woman when I was not supposed to. I was preparing for my tantric studies and as a tantric, I was not supposed to have any kind of relationship with others. But I hid my love affair with my tantric master and trained as a tantric. Soon my whole affair came out. And I was given a choice to be tantric or be a family man. I chose the former. And I asked the woman I loved to go away and not to return. Poor woman, she was heartbroken. Yet she did as I wished. She went away from me. What I didn't know then, what she didn't tell me then was that she had my child within her. That I would become a father soon. Perhaps she loved me too much. She thought if she told me about the child perhaps they would never allow me to be tantric and so she hid it from me.'

Agathashatru maintained a heavy silence. 'And a couple of years down the line when I became a tantric master myself a boy came to enrol as a tantric. The boy was an Orphan he had told. His father left him when he was still in his mother's womb and his mother died early because of an incurable disease.'

'I thought the little boy underwent a tragedy. I liked the boy he was an expert in many tantric fields. But he began to go wrong. He was keen on learning the dark tantrism. He was the one named Charvik. And on that fateful day, some 1000 years ago, when my master stopped him from completing the ritual. Did he reveal his Origins to me? He told me his mother's name. He told me that he was my son. That he was my creation. I had abandoned him as a little child, I was the reason for her mother's untimely death, I was the cause for all his sufferings. And now he returned to take his revenge from me. I never recovered from that experience.

My Master's words came back to me ' If at all you have made a choice that you know is the wrong one. Admit it and bear its consequences. Lest you will not be able to either bear the consequences or admit it.' But it was too late now. I have to rectify my mistake.'

Yajin heard it all with shock. 'Charvik is your son?'

'Yes!' Agathashatru answered, 'the last time, 300 years ago, when I tried to summon the golden warrior. Giriraj and a few others who were with me participating in the struggle realized all that I had done. They hated me for the things I had done. So, they cut all their ties with me and instead went away to find another solution to stop Charvik.'

Yajin realized now why Giriraj was adamant about giving the Golden Key to him.

They heard birds scream from far away in the sky. It was the flying beast carrying Erish headed towards them.

Erish saw the flying beast nearing an old guarded mansion. And it landed before the mansion. Two people one old and another young were at the gates of the mansion while a couple of other people were inside the doors watching intently at Erish.

Erish felt as if these people were aware that he was coming there and were waiting for him.

He landed on the ground with the Golden Sword and the Golden key. He was still not fully recovered from the blows Giriraj had gifted him. Painfully and eagerly, he went to the men to ask about the whereabouts of the Golden Warrior.

He went near Agathashatru and Yajin and kept looking at them.

'Come with us, kid!' Agathashatru said and took him inside the mansion.

Erish walked along with these men. By the looks of them, he felt he was dealing with the people he had met earlier on his journeys like Hridyanshu, Indranuj, and Bakula. These men did not speak a single word and just kept walking towards a door far away.

Finally, they reached the door. They all stood by the side-lines of the door giving space to Erish. Erish saw before him was a gigantic Golden Door. 'This is the Golden Chamber where the Golden Warrior is there' Erish thought.

In the middle of the door was a lock. Erish instinctively understood that he had to use the Golden Key to open the Golden Chamber. Quickly getting hold of the Golden Key he inserted it into the Golden Chamber and turned the key.

Erish could feel the Golden Doors shifting their gears and operating from within to open the door. He could hear the metallic noise coming from metals moving here and there within the Golden doors.

The doors slammed open and bright golden light emerged from the chamber within.

The light was so bright that Erish had to close his eyes from it.

Then the light subsided. The tantric men wore black robes and started muttering strange words when they entered the Golden Chamber and formed a circle within.

Erish didn't understand what was going on. He felt oddly scared about what was going to happen to him. He too entered the Golden Chamber looking for the Golden Warrior. He looked below the surface on which he was walking. It was emerald suited and he could see his reflection on the surface like a mirror. He observed his severely beaten face, his broken nose, and bruised cheek.

He walked and walked till he reached the centre of the Golden Chamber.

The Tantrics surrounded him in a circle and started muttering loudly in a language unknown to Erish.

Erish started floating from the ground and was levitating in mid-air.

He looked around to find out what was happening. The tantrics were absorbed in their mutterings.

Then suddenly all the tantrics directed their hands towards Erish and fire started flowing from their hands.

A big ball of golden fire came rushing at Erish in all directions and started devouring him.

Erish tried to cover himself by cocooning himself like a baby but to no use. The fire was gushing at every available opening. The heat was rising to unbearable levels. He could hear distant chants from the tantrics who were muttering something in the chorus. The fire responded to their chants.

His skin started melting with the fire. His innards started exposing themselves. He screamed and cried in pain. The pain was unbearable. Erish twisted and curled like a snake set on fire.

The fire entered inside him through his mouth, ears, and nostrils. Increasing the pain to ever new levels.

Yajin who was participating in the ritual could smell the burning flesh of the little boy. The screams of the little boy were terrible but he did not stop could not stop. If stopped in between then the ritual would fail.

He had discussed the ritual earlier with Agathashatru and all. He was shocked to hear that the boy would be burnt to ashes to summon the Golden Warrior. Then too there were no guarantees that the Golden Warrior would come. Nonetheless, they had no choice but to go with this plan. Erish had already proved that he was ready to die to save his sister.

Erish wriggled under the fire screaming madly. He could not

understand what was going on. He vaguely remembered the words of Giriraj, 'the test you will be facing ahead would be much more brutal and much more painful than what you have encountered till now.' He now understood why Giriraj was so adamant about giving the Golden Key.

Erish started to cry with pain. 'Stop! Please Stop!' But his words were melting like his tongue. His whole body was dematerializing right there and then. And he was experiencing excruciating pain.

His vision started blurring little by little. Life was choking out of him. It was more than he can endure.

Memories started rolling back in his mind in the last moments of his life. About his sister Asmi, his headmaster, and school friends. The people he met during this arduous journey. In that hell of a fire, the face of Avyay came before him. The words that Avyay told him started ringing in his ears. 'It doesn't matter how many hands you have got what matters is what you have got in the one you have got!' He also remembered the two words Avyay spoke to him almost 15 days ago.

The Ship was floating gently on the water. Avyay sat on the edge, his feet dripping in the water. He was staring blankly into the water lost in some thought.

One of the crew members came and sat gently beside Avyay so that he is not disturbed.

He asked Avyay, 'Are you still thinking of that little boy Erish?'

Avyay nodded his head without even looking at him.

'You think the boy will succeed?' the crew member asked.

'I want him to succeed,' Avyay answered.

Erish recalled the two words Avyay told him. With renewed might, He roared and came back to life. It was as if he was challenging the fire to burn him some more.

The tantrics felt the power of fire subsiding and they pushed their powers even farther and the fire once again started rushing at Erish. Erish was consuming and absorbing the fire as much as he could.

Agathashatru started laughing with madness. Yajin heard the madness in his master's laughter. Yet this laughter was not with madness but with hope. The boy withstood the final test. He refused to give up when it was most essential and the fire was powerless before him.

The Golden Warrior had been summoned.

Agathashatru recalled the conversation he had with his Master a thousand years ago.

'The price of summoning the Golden Warrior is death.' Agathashatru's Master continued, 'You…find him…will come… you searching for him…Recognize him...'

Agathashatru had spent years in search of the man who could summon the Golden Warrior all in vain. But now with the process reaching its completion, he understood what his master had meant to say that day on how to find the Golden Warrior.

'You cannot find him. He will come to you searching for himself. Recognize him when he comes.'

The ball of fire raging around Erish started to subside. He felt oddly calm. Little by little he felt his wounds heal. He felt lighter and dropped suddenly on the ground.

He opened his eyes and saw his reflection on the emerald floor.

He saw his eyes in the reflection. They were Goldeneyes!

CHAPTER 16

The Golden Chamber filled itself with the mad laughter of Agathashatru. He was crying happily. Screaming, 'The Golden Warrior has come!'

All the tantrics looked staringly at The Golden Warrior: The Warrior was born from the flames of fire!

The ritual was completed successfully.

Erish looked at himself in the reflection. There was a golden aura around him. He muscled his twisted arm. The twisted arm was no longer twisted, it was covered in gold. The entire twisted arm evolved into a powerful Golden arm.

Erish felt as if the fire was still burning in his belly.

He looked around at the tantrics who had burnt him alive. All of them were staring back at him.

Agathashatru came forward and looked him straight in the eye. 'You are The Golden Warrior!' He said.

'I am the Golden Warrior?' Erish asked him in surprise.

'Yes, Erish you are the Golden Warrior!' His Headmaster told him.

Erish was surprised to meet his headmaster in the Golden Chamber. The Headmaster was one of the hooded tantrics. 'My headmaster tried to burn me to death!' Erish thought.

'Remember the verse we all told you.' Hridyanshu came forward and lifted his hood.

All the tantrics lifted their hoods to reveal their faces. Erish saw Indranuj, Bakula, and Giriraj as well and a few unknown faces.

Hridyanshu continued:

The one who fears neither the God,

Nor the devil,

The One who fears neither the man,

Nor the beast,

He can be found by following the morning Star,

He is the one named 'The Golden Warrior!'

He's got the hands; to hold the sword,

He's got the will; to reach the goal,

He's got the feet; to scale the see,

He's got the strength; to reach the peak,

He can be found by crossing the mount,

He's the one named 'The Golden Warrior!'

The one who fears neither the day

Nor the night,

The one who fears neither the sky

Nor the storm,

He's the one holding the Golden Sword,

He can be found by crossing the

Seven seas,

He's the one named 'The Golden Warrior!'

' The one who refuses to give up,

Even when he is fallen,

The one who stands up,

Even when he is beaten,

He can be found by following the moon,

He's the one named 'The Golden Warrior!'

' The one who brings hope,

When hope is chopped,

The one who brings life,

When life is choked.

He can be found by crossing death,

He is the one named the Golden Warrior!'

Hridyanshu completed his Verse. Boy, it was you all along. You were the Golden Warrior! You defeated the Asin! You crossed the mountain and surpassed the seven seas. It was you who held the Golden sword. It was you who brought hope when hope was lost.

Even when you were choked to death by the fire you brought back your life. You are the Golden Warrior!

Erish could feel the power within himself. As if he was connected to a power source then would never run out of power.

Still, his head was so full of questions. 'How come you all are here?' he asked, 'Do you know each other?'

Giriraj answered with a smile on his face, 'We can be anywhere we chose! We are tantrics!'

'And for your second question,' Agathashatru said, 'It so happened that the last time when I tried to summon the Golden Warrior. The ritual did not perform and the man died. So, some of my students had an altercation with me on how to find the Golden Warrior? They left me and went on their way to find the Golden Warrior and to stop Charvik by other means. Some of them were Great Grandfathers of Bakula, Indranuj, Hridyanshu, and your Headmaster. They vowed to stop Charvik without going the way I had outlined for my way did fail so many times. And they did succeed my boy. They have finally found the Golden Warrior. That is, you.'

'But why did all of you lie to me that there is a Golden Warrior? When there was no Golden Warrior?' Erish asked.

'Because had we told you then that there is no Golden Warrior, that there is no one who can save your sister, that Charvik cannot be stopped,' Giriraj answered, ' then you wouldn't have persevered as you did. People need hope. You needed that hope that there is someone out there by the name of the Golden Warrior who could save your sister. Without that hope, you wouldn't have fought the Asin, crossed the mountain, pulled the Golden Sword, or Sail the seven seas. Only on that hope did you do all those things.'

Erish let those words sink in.

'We don't have much time Erish! Charvik would initiate the ritual in an hour. We have Asmi and others to save. Let's get their quick.' Headmaster said.

All the tantrics muttered some strange sayings and birds with gigantic frames started landing outside the mansion.

All the tantrics climbed the birds. While Erish climbed the flying beast. Yajin and Agathashatru climbed Ovin, the Owl. And were on their way to save Asmi and stop Charvik.

Giriraj led the way. Charvik had told him 15 days ago, 'You know where to find me.' Charvik would be at the sacrificial altar.

Giriraj's disciple who was behind him on the same gigantic bird asked the tantrics, 'I want to know how come you all are alive for 1000 years?'

'My disciples are loyal to me,' Agathashatru answered, 'They died for me so that I can extend my life to stop Charvik.'

' **I**nitiate the rituals and bring all the sacrifices.' Charvik ordered, 'No one can stop me now!'

Mahakethu took the orders and proceeded to line up all the three hundred kids at the sacrificial altar. Asmi along with others was dragged out of their cells and brought to the sacrificial altar.

Lava surrounded the entire sacrificial altar. The whole atmosphere was heated. Charvik's followers were ready at their respective places with big black choppers. Their places were marked with strange symbols and writings.

They were chorus muttering some mantras. They all proceeded to start the rituals when there was a big blast from a corner of the sacrificial altar.

Charvik saw upwards as gigantic birds started dropping below and he saw his father Agathashatru land before him.

Something crept in Charvik's mind at the sight of his father. He could see guilt in his father's eyes. He was responsible after all for all the misery Charvik had to go through. And here he was for the final time trying to stop him.

Besides Agathashatru, Giriraj landed and looked at Charvik. Charvik saw his one-time favourite teacher trying one last time to do what he failed to do three times earlier.

And there were also some other men besides them. But no one not even one could have the power to battle Charvik. Agathashatru's Master was the last Tantric who could have stopped Charvik but with him gone none was equivalent to Charvik's power.

Charvik had a faint wicked smile on his lips. 'So, you think you can stop me this time?'

'No, we don't. But there is someone who can!' Giriraj answered mysteriously.

'Who is it?' Charvik challenged.

Agathashatru answered, 'The one who was supposed to stop you. The Warrior born from the flames of fire.'

'Oh! You mean the Golden Warrior?' Charvik said spitefully, 'Show me your Golden Warrior.'

Just then the flying beast landed between them. And Erish stepped down.

Charvik remembered the little boy who had thrown a stone at him when he was taking Asmi from the school. The same boy, Aghori had shown him. The one who was searching for the mythical Golden Warrior.

Asmi who was held down by an Outsider looked at Erish and screamed, 'Erish!'

Erish saw Asmi tied down by an Outsider and anger was building up in his veins.

Charvik shot a glance at Asmi and Erish. Going near Asmi he bent down he said, 'Seems your little brother did come to save you?'

Charvik ordered his men, 'All of you line up. Kill the tantrics first then we will complete the ritual.'

The Outsiders lined up against Charvik as the tantrics lined up against Erish.

All of them started releasing balls of fire and blasts from their hands. Giriraj took his long sword and started to take on Mahakethu who was using his big black chopper for the fight.

Agathashatru, Indranuj, Bakula, Hridyanshu all were battling two or more Outsiders at once.

Pandemonium erupted all over the Sacrificial altar. Kids started running helter-skelter into a corner to escape the exploding blasts.

While all this was happening, Charvik and Erish were staring at each other. Charvik took one step closer and raised his head high to take a closer look at the puny little Golden Warrior.

With a faint smile, Charvik took his big black chopper and rushed at Erish. Erish prepared himself and took the Golden Sword from his scabbard and blocked Charvik's attack. Sparkles were flying everywhere as Charvik's and Erish's sword collided with each other.

Charvik was not able to land even a single blow. He jumped backward and put his sword down.

Asmi was looking at Erish and Charvik from a corner. Charvik closed his eyes and muttered something. Charviks's shadow raised from the ground and clutched to Charvik's body and Charvik with a pitch-black shadow against him started growing ever bigger in size and strength.

Agathashatru had told Erish earlier, 'By the use of Dark Tantrism, Charvik had ended his human form and turned half diabolical in his being. That is why no Tantric no matter how powerful was ever able to stop him. When you fight him, he will reveal his diabolical form at that time you need to use the full power of the Golden Warrior to defeat him Only then can he be defeated and you could save your sister.'

Erish instantly held the sword in both his hands horizontally and muttered, 'By the powers vested in me, I command the Golden Powers to come to my aid in full powers!'

As soon as Erish completed his Mantra. A Golden Aura started eclipsing him. His shadow got up from behind him and clutched to him. And he too started growing ever bigger as the size of Charvik.

Now both Charvik and Erish took flight in the air. Erish used his Golden Sword and readied himself all the while watching the diabolical form of Charvik. Charvik's eyes were turned in pitch black and his skin was getting darker and darker.

Two figures were looming above the sacrificial altar. One Golden, the other Blackish.

Erish and Charvik attacked each other with their respective armoury. Erish's Golden Sword matched Charvik's dark Chopper.

Their swords were held in struggling positions. All the while, Charvik's strength was exceeding to ever greater heights. Erish was not able to withhold his position for long and Charvik overcame him.

Charvik dealt Erish a series of blows and kicked him down to the ground. No sooner had Erish fallen did Charvik brought the Chopper at his head. In time, Erish grabbed his sword and blocked Charvik's attack.

'So, this all you have got Golden Warrior?' Charvik echoed his voice in diabolical form.

Charvik's face was as close to Erish as it could get. Erish saw his dark form. His bulging crooked wolf-like teeth and blackish eyes. And Erish was scared at the sight of Charvik.

Erish's hands were shaking with fear. He did not believe he could defeat Charvik. While Charvik grew ever harder on Erish.

Just then Erish heard a familiar voice. 'Remember what I told you on the day we departed,' Avyay said, 'Remember the words I spoke to you.'

The sight of Avyay and his words raised hopes in Erish. Erish remembered the words Avyay spoke to him. He recalled the two words which helped him navigate so many trying circumstances. He recalled those two words that gave him so much power when he little had it.

'Tell me those words, Erish,' Avyay said.

Erish roared with fury, 'STAND UP!'

With all the might he could muster. He roared back to life pushing Charvik from him. Erish felt renewed energy passing through him.

Avyay motivated Erish, 'That diabolical being,' Avyay said pointing to Charvik, ' wants to kill your sister. Would you let it happen?'

'NO!' Erish screamed.

'Then go finish him off once for and all!' Avyay shouted.

Charvik took his big black chopper and Erish regained his composure with the Golden Sword.

Both took a moment to prepare themselves and came running towards each other.

Their swords collided mightily in between spending dark and gold sparks everywhere. Erish disarmed Charvik of his sword and thrusted the Golden sword in Charvik's belly.

The Golden Sword unleashed its unfathomable powers. Bright Gold Light was spreading throughout the place. Charvik roared in pain and defeat.

Everyone closed their eyes unable to withstand the bright golden light. All the followers of Charvik were vanishing along with Charvik in the Golden light.

Little by little the gold light subsided. Asmi opened her eyes looking intently at the place where Charvik and Erish collided.

Only one was standing in that location and that was Erish.

After a moment's lapse, Erish fell to his knees and fell to the ground. Erish was unable to understand what was happening to him. He felt all the powers inside him leaving him. He could feel the fire in his belly dying. Tiny little golden sparks were glowing from him.

Asmi came running shouting, 'Erish!'

Agathashatru, Giriraj, Avyay, and the rest of them came for Erish's aid.

Asmi held her tiny brother Erish in her lap.

Erish opened his eyes. He saw Avyay with a crying face. Avyay was crying. Avyay kneeled before Erish and waved his hand over Erish's cheeks.

Erish asked, 'Am I going to die?'

Avyay nodded his head.

Asmi said, 'No! Erish!'

Giriraj's disciple remembered what Giriraj had told him earlier, 'Sooner or later, in one way or another the boy will die.'

The disciple now realised that the price of summoning the Golden Warrior's powers was death.

Yajin who was observing this all suddenly became aware of the sparkles rising from Agathshatru.

'Master!' Yajin shuddered.

Agathashtru who had waited more than a thousand years to stop his son finally succeeded.

'There is no more need for me here Yajin. I should have been dead long ago but I postponed it and others had paid the price for my longevity. But not anymore. I too am going to Yajin. Take care of yourself.' Agathashatru said, 'Shwetakethu, I name you as my successor. Take care of all.'

Saying so, even Agathashtru vanished along with Erish.

Asmi cried and cried for her little brother who came so far to save her. But all her tears could not stop from Erish vanishing from her arms.

CHAPTER 18

Two tiny tots one girl and another boy were playing along the riverside when one of them saw a never before seen object flowing from the river.

The tiny boy went running into the river and caught that strange object.

His sister was asking to share the toy with her but the boy refused and went running towards their mom to make her see the strange object.

The boy asked his mother, 'What's this Mum?'

Their mother saw the object and replied, 'It's a Rakhi!'

'What's a Rakhi?' the boy questioned.

'A Rakhi is a promise that a brother always protects his sister.'

The boy said, 'I found it flowing the river.'

'It means,' the mother answered, 'that somewhere a little boy like you protected his sister!'

www.ingramcontent.com/pod-product-compliance
Lightning Source LLC
LaVergne TN
LVHW091503170726
843492LV00001B/310